A Place of Ravens

A Place of Ravens

Pamela Hill

ST. MARTIN'S PRESS • NEW YORK

Library of Congress Cataloging in Publication Data

Hill, Pamela.
     A place of ravens.

     I.   Title.
'PR6058.I446P57   823'.914   80-28045
ISBN 0-312-61373-3

A Place of Ravens

ONE

She peered through the narrow slit between the close-drawn curtains of Aunt Elizabeth Talmadge's antique litter, surveying what could be seen of the summer roads. She would sooner have ridden them; she could ride well, and the distance would not have been too great. But Aunt Talmadge—who truth to tell was not strictly an aunt but Dad's second cousin—grudged the price of feeding and watering an extra horse and had insisted that they travel together in this awkward, lumbering equipage. However the journey would soon be done, and then—

Clemency lowered her dark-tipped lashes, trying not to show the excitement that was rising in her. She knew very well that Aunt Talmadge and Dad had arranged this marriage to suit themselves, but there might be some diversion in it; Dad would not have pledged her to it else. Dear Dad with his handsome, coarsening blond looks, his reckless losses at cards and in the tennis-court, where he had once beaten the Prince of Wales despite his age—Dad with his fine deep voice that could sing roundelays as well as any of the younger courtiers, so that unsuitable ladies were always falling in love with him—Dad hoped that she, Clemency, would make good some of the losses by contriving this fine marriage that Aunt Talmadge hoped to bring about, marvellously come to hand although Dad could provide no dowry.

Clemency knew very well that her own looks made up for lack of riches; many had already told her so despite her youth. The world-weary woman who lay opposite on the cushions surveyed her beneath narrowed lids. Mark Holles' daughter, she was thinking, was indeed a beauty; the silver-gilt hair, falling to Clemency's calves when it was loosed, had been hoisted on a frame for this journey, so as to seem fashionable. The hazel eyes, under their arched fine brows, looked out from beneath a bared forehead smooth as a snowdrift; and her mouth, as one of the young men at Court had said with small inspiration, was like a ruby, her teeth like pearls. Her nose was straight, and with the proud flaring nostrils and stubborn, piquant chin presented a face that no man would readily subdue. Moreover she was slender and straight like a young tree, and her breasts already repaid showing in the immodest low-cut bodices the Queen had made fashionable. Aunt Talmadge had however decreed a high-necked gown for today, and it chafed Clemency in the hot weather. She hoped that she would please her bridegroom at sight, for none of the poetic young men had made her an offer. Also, she was too young to remain at Court without Alice, her sister, who had recently eloped with Gregory Savernake. "By the time Dad found them they were bedded," Clemency was thinking, "and Savernake hath no money any more than Alice. God knoweth what will become of them, but the King thought it a great jest." King James had in fact thrust his sad-eyed face with its slobbering mouth towards the bride, saying she was a fair young wench and he would have liked to be in the bride-groom's place. But everyone knew he preferred young men. Perhaps he would make Alice and Gregory a bride-gift to enable them to start life together. Whatever befell, it made it all the more urgent that she, Clemency, should marry well, and where better than at this country house called Ravensyard, whose young lord, Nicholas Talmadge, needed a wife?

Her mind skimmed over the young man's name, for she had

no face to put to it. Any questions she had asked her aunt had met strict rejoinders as to what was or was not becoming in a young maid, telling her nothing. Perhaps Aunt was mortified at having again to set eyes on her second husband John Talmadge, from whom she had been parted these fifteen years and who was Nicholas' guardian. Well, it could not be helped; but the name of Ravensyard was itself intriguing.

"Tell me again, good aunt, of the ravens."

"Will the child never be done? I have told you four times. There have been ravens at Ravensyard from time immemorial, and it is said that if they ever leave it, evil will triumph." Aunt Talmadge closed her small shrewd eyes again and fell into a pretended doze on the cushions. Small, dark, shrewd and somewhat terrifying, Aunt Talmadge; what had fallen out between her and her husband? His name was John, and he had stayed on at Ravensyard to have an eye to the boy Nicholas, whose father had fallen in the Dutch wars in the old Queen's time. It did not sound as though young Nicholas would himself have to go a-soldiering; since the King came down from Scotland to unite the two thrones, there had been peace.

"Tell me more of my husband," she begged of the sleeping face. Aunt Talmadge opened her eyes again and frowned.

"Can you not have patience till you see him? Nick dotes on his books, that is all I can say; I have not seen him myself since he was at the breast. Your uncle loves him well enough."

"Well enough to leave you to your own devices in London?"

" 'Twas I who left him, for I cannot endure the country. Have done with your pert questioning, and wait till you may see for yourself."

Clemency relapsed into silence; after all, what she had learned was not displeasing. She also liked to read; she loved rhyming songs and lute-playing. Would Nicholas Talmadge like such things? She dared not ask.

She must have looked enquiring still, because Aunt Talmadge suddenly said "At all events, comport yourself with dignity," which left one with the feeling of having been slapped. Clemency almost rebelled; after all, she wasn't a bride yet. It remained to be seen whether or not she and Nick Talmadge dealt well together: Dad had promised that. But perhaps it would be like Dad's other promises, unsubstantial as air, like the time he had promised her a pomander and a blue silk gown, and then forgotten. Supposing she and Nick misliked one another? It would surely then be folly to wed. But other weddings had been so made, especially where there was money. She suppressed a shiver, lest the older woman see it and make her put on her cloak again. How hot it was! The litter smelt of Aunt Talmadge, of age and sweat and lavender. She smiled winningly; it would pass the time to make Aunt Talmadge talk, whether she would or no. "Tell me again," Clemency said, "of Ravensyard."

"Yet more torment! I have told you a-many times, and now you may wait till you see it." Nevertheless she went on, as though despite herself she were proud of the house's history. "'Twas taken from the Welsh in my great-grandfather's time, and Talmadges have held it ever since." The sentence ended abruptly, for Elizabeth had borne no children by her second marriage to John Talmadge. But there was the beautiful and, Dad said, dangerous jade Marguerite from Aunt's first marriage with John Liston. Marguerite lived nearby Ravensyard. Perhaps she would be there to greet them, if her husband, who Aunt said was disagreeable, let her come. It was impossible not to ask.

"Will Marguerite be there to greet us?"

Elizabeth Talmadge never minded speaking of her daughter. She sat up in stiff pride, like a rooster; her ruff, which was set in the old high fashion, made it impossible to ease her neck.

"Marguerite must do as she is bid, for Peter Hautboys loveth not the Talmadge clan. But one day soon you will see her; and there are others there to whom you must have an eye; Joan Talmadge and her sons."

"I have heard you speak of them."

"I cannot tell you too often, for they are a danger. Dick is a lecher and hath good looks; beware of him, and still more of Ralph, who is a plotter for his own advancement. Their mother

Joan is worse than either, though their father, God be praised, is dead. They will come without doubt to try to meddle with the marriage, for Joan likes ill to see Ravensyard pass from her heirship, she having married her own cousin withal. You had best solve that riddle by bearing a son to Nick."

So I must bear as well as marry, and it is in truth all settled, Clemency thought. The mention of Dame Joan was a challenge, enough to make one settle for the marriage. Why oppose it in any case? Even were Nick Talmadge a hunchback, or afflicted with spots, Ravensyard was a fine house and there was plenty of money.

Clemency resumed her staring at the curtains. "Aunt, may I not draw them back for coolness?" The summer heat was stifling, and her hands and the place between her shoulder-blades were sticky with sweat. But Aunt Talmadge only frowned, and shook her frizzed head.

"We do not want the common folk to gaze on us as we pass, saying to one another that there goes the Talmadge bride. Remember that the name is a great and ancient one and every-thing you do will be noted; we are not at the rumbustious Court any longer, changed sadly as that hath been from the good Queen's day."

"Except for the King's fancies, who are better than any," Clemency whipped out, then regretted it; one should not mention those young men in front of an ageing dame who remembered the great days of Queen Bess. Aunt Talmadge's mouth primmed up and she was silent. I know too much for a young maid, thought Clemency; she has told me so time and again. If my mother had lived I would have been kept more closely, and so would Alice.

She endured the silence, and to console herself tried to think, forgetting the litter swaying in the heat, of the time long ago when she and Alice, children both, had danced before the old Queen. The lean face, painted with white lead, had watched them out of eyes that still shone like opals despite the lack of brows or lashes. Their dancing had diverted Her Grace, for she had still been broken-hearted over Essex, her favourite who had

11

been executed in the previous year. Folk said it killed her in the end. But she had spoken with the two children after their dance, a sign that she was pleased. "When I was your age I danced by myself, for there was none to dance with me," she said. "Later, when I was grown, the Spanish Ambassador wrote to his King about my dancing, which they said was very fine." And she had dismissed them with a smile which showed her black teeth, and had later paid much heed to Dad, though she gave him nothing. But Clemency would always remember the stiff bejewelled figure seated like a great doll in its chair of state. The Queen's wit had been sharper than a doll's, as everyone knew; but now she was dead and instead, the King had come down from Scotland with his great sad eyes and dribbling mouth and weak legs, and later his Danish Queen Anne, who at one time had made much of Clemency until she forgot about her. But taken all in all the Court was no place for a maid now, as even Dad admitted; and swiftly, after the disgrace of Alice, had come Aunt Talmadge's plan for this marriage with her husband's kin.

"There is the house now," said the older woman suddenly, peering through the curtain-slit. "They will be watching for us; sit up and smooth your hair." She herself seemed much agitated; was it because of meeting her estranged lord, or because of Dame Joan, who was surely there to work ill?

So it was in summer daylight that Clemency first saw Ravens-yard, and she drew a breath of enchantment.

Never had she seen so beautiful a house. It was not built in the new style with terraces and gardens and chimneys of carved brick; rather it was like a fortress, secret and swirling upwards from its high containing wall towards turrets and hidden places beyond. Its sheen, with the sun upon it, was gold, for the stones were lichened; perhaps on dark days the house would look grey, but there was still the secrecy and grandeur. Clemency hardly saw the road, the river, the clustered cottages and thin trees descending at last to form a spinney where the shade was thick. She could think of nothing beyond the house itself. Nick Talmadge might be wood-mad, squinting or afflicted in any way

12

anyone chose; she would marry him for the sake of this house. It must be hers, it must!

She dragged her gaze back to meet Dame Elizabeth's narrow regard. The older woman might have read her thoughts. "There is hardly such another now in England, I believe," she said, "they have all been pulled down to make way for mullions and pleasances and kickshaws. But here they might hold siege as in times of old; few could breach that wall."

"May they never have to do so," Clemency laughed. She was very happy. But Aunt Talmadge did not return her smile.

"Ravensyard may descend to heirs-male only," she said, as if it were of no consequence.

The litter carried them up the rise and to a door in the wall. Aunt Talmadge clapped her hands for the driver to halt. "Best alight here, and the beasts can be led round for watering," she said. Clemency found herself climbing out as stiffly as an old woman after the cramping journey. They went through the door; she was so intent on staring at the house that Aunt Talmadge had to touch her on the arm to bring her back to the fact that they were not only expected, but curtsied to. The Ravensyard servants had come out, decked in their best stiffened linen now starch could be got everywhere. Clemency noted their curious eyes and one or two of their faces; a tall woman with dark eyes she remembered, and a little bowing man who looked like a Frenchman. She smiled gaily. They have accepted me, she was thinking, and I have accepted Ravensyard. The rest doth not matter.

They had crossed the small inner courtyard beyond the gate and had reached the entry-door, set cornerwise above steps. Company waited there; it was already possible to guess who everyone might be. A stooped man in his fifties, with a narrow cautious face, came forward; this was Aunt Talmadge's husband. Despite their long parting husband and wife kissed coolly, then Clemency found herself under the scrutiny of John Talmadge's cold blue eyes. She made her curtsy, and did not let her glance fall; look for look, she thought, and neither will be

13

master. He seemed pleased enough, and led her forward to where a tall commanding woman in unfashionable clothes, with a rose-leaf complexion and fading golden hair, stood with her two sons in the shadow beyond the door. This could be none but Dame Joan, John Talmadge's sister who had married her cousin. Brother and sister had a resemblance, more in expression than feature; John Talmadge could never have been called handsome, whereas Dame Joan was still beautiful, and knew it. She was proud as well; she scarcely bent her head to acknowledge the bride, regarding her expressionlessly out of eyes hard as sapphires as though she, and not Joan herself, were the interloper. The two young men stayed by her; presently the elder, a strikingly handsome tall well-made youth, bent low over Clemency's hand. This is the lecher, she thought; as well be warned. "Have done with your French manners, Dick," said his mother curtly. The young man stood up and his blue eyes, like his mother's but a trifle too prominent, roved over Clemency and lingered on her breasts. At least he acts no part, she thought. Joan presented her second son, Ralph, who was darker and less forward; he kept his eyes on the ground. He was slighter than his brother and seemed to stand in his shadow. No one was dressed in the height of fashion, and Clemency no longer felt outmoded in her high-necked gown. Was there not some tale Aunt Talmadge had told her about Joan's falling foul of the old Queen long ago? It would not have been difficult to displease that exacting lady, especially if one were a woman. But where was Nicholas Talmadge, her bridegroom? She had well-nigh forgotten him at sight of these folk.

She saw him then. He stood even more deeply in the shadows than Ralph, as if Joan's welcome had foremost right; by him was a tall dark servant. Clemency looked at Nicholas Talmadge; she saw a young man of middle height, very thin, white-cheeked as though he never went outdoors, and with a weak mouth the colour of a rose. His glance wavered and he did not seem at ease. "Come, Nick, kiss thy bride," said John Talmadge heavily. "She has ridden far to do your pleasure."

The young man came obediently and pecked Clemency on

the cheek, blushing as he did so. His mouth felt cool to the touch and she was sorry for him. This marriage would be strange to him also; she would do her best to atone, for was not the house the prize? He had gentle brown eyes, long-lashed, she had noticed; she was sure he would never hurt any living thing. She smiled after his kiss and tried, shyly, to respond to the feeling there ought to be springing between them. But it did not seem real; nothing was real but Ravensyard.

TWO

"Where are the ravens? I was told that they are always here."

"They nest on the roof. Master Nicholas makes a pet of one."

Clemency lay back and allowed the maid to go on threading the comb through her loosened hair. She was somewhat heady with the wine she had been given to drink, and pleased with herself, with life and with the house. She would never be done asking questions until she knew everything they could tell her.

"What is your name?" she asked the maid, who was deft and had been given to her for herself. They had told her, and she had forgotten; it was the wine. But the woman showed no sign of offence. She was the tall dark one Clemency had noted on entering.

"Emma Theale, mistress. I am married to Theale the baker here. I was a Penellyn."

She spoke as if the name signified. Clemency, eased now that her stiff bodice and farthingale had been loosed till dinner-time, stretched a little, pleasurably. "Is that a common name hereabouts?" she asked, to be agreeable; the woman had spoken as if she were a queen in her linen apron.

"It is not common."

The resolute lips folded and for the first time Clemency looked at the woman and forgot the servant. Besides her height she was, one had to admit, somewhat fierce in her appearance, having the look almost of a falcon with its dark eyes hooded. Which one had been the husband, Theale? It was good that they had their own baker. There was so much she must find out and know before becoming mistress here, for neither John Talmadge nor his sister should get the better of her, she was resolved. John had been deferential enough, ushering her to the twisting stairs which led to this room, and sending Emma Theale to tend her. "I am treated as though I had brought a dowry," she thought, and knowing the ways of the world this fact nagged at her; why should they be so pleased to see her? Nicholas Talmadge, with his ancient name and his gold, could surely have looked higher.

Where else had she seen Emma Theale's face? It seemed familiar.

Suddenly she knew. In the bustle of arrival she had hardly taken note of him, yet now she remembered; the tall servant who stood by Nicholas in the shadows. Emma Theale spread out her hair for her in a shining veil. "Have you kin in the house?" Clemency asked. "Methought I saw one who looked as you do, down in the hall."

"That is my brother, David Penellyn, who looketh to Master Nicholas."

So she had been right, even in one small matter. She longed to ask the maid more, but it would not be seemly; she would find out through Aunt Talmadge of her husband. She twirled a lock of her silver-gilt hair round her finger, tucked the matter of the Penellyns away in her mind and tried to think of Nicholas, her betrothed; but his features had faded in her memory and she saw only David Penellyn's. Perhaps by dinner Nick would have shed his shyness; she would ask him about his raven. Sooner or later they must grow to be at ease in one another's company.

Nicholas and she were placed next to one another at the high table which was still kept as of old time; the servants ate in the lower part of the hall. Dame Joan was down a place, which did not please her; and John Talmadge sat beside his wife. They said little, but Joan's high harsh voice droned on; many beautiful women had harsh voices. Clemency took time to reflect on what she had been told in the litter, that this woman desired Ravensyard for her sons, and would go to any lengths to get it. She, Clemency, must bear a son soon in order that their ambition might fail. She stole a glance at Joan's two; both sat further down the table, Dick wolfing his food and Ralph pecking at it. Beside her, poor Nick—she already thought of him as poor Nick—ate sparingly, pulling each morsel apart as if he relished nothing. Yet it was a good enough game pie. She found a thing to say to him, and turned to ask if he had hunted the game.

He answered without looking at her, his eyes on his plate. "No, I neither hunt nor hawk." He sounded breathless, as if it were daring of him to have said as much. Someone hath kept him strictly, she thought; no doubt Master John. She said gently "What doth it please you best to do?"

"To read in my study, when I am let." Although the remark sounded churlish his voice was soft. She began to talk to him of books, of which Dad had taught her much, for he loved reading and news of curious things. Had Nicholas a herbal? She wold like to grow a herb-garden here. Had he Master Edmund Spenser's poems, Dr Donne's?

"All these, and I have the volumes of Master Shakespeare's plays and sonnets, and the Book of Hours of the Duc d'Orléans, and a bestiary."

"And a pet raven."

He smiled for the fifirst time. "Yes, it will take bread from my hand."

It would be easy to grow fond of him, she had decided. "You love beasts and birds, as you will not kill them," she said. Their eyes met as his glance flickered quickly upwards, then down again to his plate.

"All God's creatures," he said in a low voice.

Clemency was pleased, for it showed they had something in common; she had always hated the shedding of blood, and the

19

tale of the deer Queen Bess had let go free after cutting its ears off; to stroke a bird's feathers, to let a cat walk by one's skirts and sun itself, were greater pleasures. Perhaps she could have a pet dog at Ravensyard, a little creature to carry on her arm. Perhaps—

John Talmadge leant over with misplaced heartiness. "You are deep in talk so soon? That is as it should be; I am glad to see it. Do you know, Mistress Clemency, that our Nick hath never yet looked on a wench? I hope you may teach him otherwise. The fellow is in luck with so fair a bride."

Poor Nick fell silent, and Clemency felt her cheeks redden. There were eyes watching here, as there had always been at Court; it was no different, only smaller. After they had all gone off and she and Nicholas had the house to themselves, it would be different. If only Aunt Talmadge would take her husband back to London! There was small hope of that, she knew; they had gone their separate ways too long; yet they seemed to be dealing well enough together now, and they had written to one another over the years. How many deep currents, like a smooth stream between its banks, swirled about the high table! That there was hate she was certain, some of it for herself.

After the meal they called upon her to dance. That was Aunt Talmadge's fault; she had always liked to show off Clemency and Alice as though they were performing animals, and Alice was not here to give support. The lower trestles had been cleared away and a shout went up for the man Penellyn. He had left the hall at the clearing; now he returned with a small harp, plucking the strings and tuning them. The notes were sweet and plaintive, more plangent than those of a lute, but they would serve. She matched herself to their rhythm, spreading her skirts in the prescribed manner of a pavon, and dancing the steps. The harp's swept strings echoed in her ears and she began to take fire from them; then she remembered all the eyes upon her and continued seemly beneath the cold gaze of Dame Joan and the hot one of Dick, and the rest. Aunt Talmadge sat nodding approvingly, like a mother hen. If only Alice were here!

Loneliness overcame the bride in this strange hall; if only Alice's familiar white fingers clasped hers she would be at ease, but to dance alone was strange . . . She would write to Alice as soon as might be. The enchantment had fled from the music; casting a glance at the high table she saw Nicholas was not watching her, but staring at his knees below the trestle's edge.

Yet she was watched by another. Clemency suddenly became aware of the gaze of David Penellyn like a dark flame above his harp. A servant! It would never do. Her cheeks flushed hotly and she curtsied formally, and returned to the applause of the high table. Even Dame Joan drawled a compliment, and said she had danced well. But Nick said nothing, and nobody pressed him to speak; it was as if they had all forgotten him.

That night Clemency shared her bed with Aunt Talmadge, who continued her watchfu silence; it meant Clemency had pleased well enough. She did not ask the girl what she thought of her bridegroom and Clemency was glad of it; she had not yet fully made up her mind about Nick; there was some hidden matter she did not understand, and she did not care to ask concerning it.

However there were other questions one might ask; she spoke of the Penellyns.

"They do not seem like servants, but almost as though they owned the house and we were guests in it; or so it seemed to me." She was, she admitted to herself, spiteful; why there was any need to be so was not clear.

Aunt Talmadge smiled wryly beneath her nightcap. "If that is the way it seemeth to them, they have small chance to make much of't; your uncle could have them whipped from the place, and they know it. They carry out their duties well enough."

"But who are they?"

"Their kin owned Ravensyard in time gone. There are many such folk in great houses nowadays, after the wars when everything changed hands. For our part, the first Ralph Talmadge fought for King Henry IV and won the land and the house in reward. As time passed the Penellyns—their name is a bastard

21

form of ap Llewelyn, for they believe themselves to be of the blood of the old Welsh princes—the Penellyns sank to become mere peasantry, then some were offered places about the house, where you see them today. If your maid puts on airs, birch her."

"She hath done naught to merit that," said Clemency quickly; the thought of birching tall Emma Theale filled her with laughter. "Who is Emma's husband?" she asked.

"Lord, how should I know them all? Yet I mind hearing of that; no matter; he is surely the baker, a little strutting cocksparrow of a man whom you may not have noticed welcoming you. He baked tonight's loaves and pastry. All these matters you must familiarise yourself with, for we cannot have Dame Joan reproaching you or trying to take your duties from you."

"But she doth not live here, surely?"

"No, but she would like to. They ride over twice a week from their dwelling, Marshalhall. Best be firm with them from the beginning; given an inch they will take an ell."

"I will remember."

After Clemency slept there came a scratching at the door and John Talmadge entered, in his bedgown.

"Not asleep, Bess? I had hoped as much, for I longed for a word alone with you though we no longer share a bed together."

"We never should have shared one; we were not of like mind, and are not now. What would you with me?"

"To talk of the bridal." He glanced at the sleeping Clemency. "Meseems we should wed them soon, before certain things may come. You have told her nothing of Nick's state?"

"Nothing, as you commanded; though she is wise enough."

"She had best find out later, if at all; marriage may cure him. They dealt well enough at supper."

"Well, this is the best match that may be made for her, my cousin being what he is, gay as a lark without two pence to rub together. He is well loved at Court, but gets no gain from that."

"What gear have you brought with her? Hath she enough shifts, gowns, shoes?" He lifted the candle he held until he could look on Clemency clearly; her lashes did not stir, and her

22

lips were parted to show her small even teeth. "How fair she is!" he said.

"She hath little but what she stands up in, having outgrown the rest. If I am to fit her out, I must have money."

"No need; when they are wed we will furnish her with gear. As the mistress of Ravensyard she should be seen richly apparelled; it is a task we might give to Joan." He smiled grimly. "How are her courses?" he asked, while Clemency's hair glittered on the pillow in the candlelight. "May they marry within days?"

"Within the week; naught to hinder."

"Then I'll see the clergyman."

"Do so. Marguerite may come tomorrow. Clemency took a liking to the house, I could tell, and will relish the ordering of it; she knows such housekeeping as I've contrived to teach her between masque-conceits and pavons and galliards. There's small quiet at Court."

"You were ever a good, comfortable housekeeper, and I never so well served since," he said. Suddenly he took her hand and kissed it. "Joan chided Dick for his French manners today, and I ape them; but it is overlong since we met. It may be that with this bridal to come, we will meet the oftener."

"You are well enough in your state, and I in mine, John; we never dealt together, and I would miss the gossip of town."

"As you will," he said evenly. Suddenly a grin split his face. "Did you mark Joan tonight, the rage well-nigh consuming her while that pretty chit danced, and the thought rising in everyone's mind that Nick may yet father sons on her? Joan lusteth for Ravensyard more than all the world."

"And hath passed on her lusts to her heir. I scarce saw him take his eyes from Clemency's breasts all of the evening."

"He is thus with any wench; it will pass, when she becomes Nick's bride."

"Guard her well, for all of that. Nick would be no stout guard, but there is the man Penellyn. She asked me tonight concerning them, and knoweth their state."

John Talmadge frowned. "Penellyn can wrestle and throw,

that is true; but Joan hath the advantage of being womanly."

"Such misliking between a brother and sister I never knew."

"'Tis worse between husband and wife," said John Talmadge, and took his leave.

The day before her marriage John Talmadge escorted Clemency from attic to cellar of Ravensyard. It was as though he were trying to say "Do not think that you make a poor bargain with this marriage." She did not think so; the sun shone, glowing on the waxy surfaces of old wood well cared for, old hangings lovingly brushed; each twisting staircase and sun-soaked room stayed in her mind like cells in a hive; parts of Ravensyard were very old. She heard her skirts' stuff brush the walls that lined the narrow passages, and her slippers sound on the flags. Other women must have come as brides to be shown all this, Talmadge brides whose portraits, some of them roughly painted by travelling limners, hung on the panelling or, as in the case of one girl in a lace wimple, were part of the panels themselves. She felt the past crowd about her; pride filled her that this house was to be hers, that she would be mistress of it, have charge of the beeswax and lavender for the furnishings and linen, hold the keys to the still-room and buttery and spice-cupboard. "It will be the easier for you," John Talmadge said, "in that all the servants have been with us long, and know the ways in which matters are conducted here."

By him, or by me? she thought, meeting his considering gaze. No doubt he thought that, as a green girl, she would take his advice. Well, so she would, for he was wise in his own ways; but she would not be prevented from having her own. "I am glad that I too know how matters are conducted, for Aunt Talmadge took much pains to teach me," she said with apparent innocence, remembering how she had carefully listened to everything while Alice, mind idle, strummed mostly at a lute. "Show me the ravens," she said mischievously; she saw his face grow cold.

"There is an entry to the roof from a trap-door, but it is not safe and it might disturb the nests to go out," he said, and shortly excused himself and went back to his office, where he worked most of the day. Clemency did not trouble to disobey him and go to look at the ravens' nests; that would be childish, she decided, and she was anxious to show John Talmadge and everyone else here that she was neither a child nor a fool. She returned to the hall, and sat by the fire which still blazed there although it was summer. So old a house must be kept warm.

THREE

"I should have liked a new gown to be wed in."

She stood and frowned, regarding the old green satin in which she had travelled here, furbished as it was with a freshly starched and laundered ruff but still, to her thinking, not fine enough for a bride, and outmoded. And she had no jewel to wear; Dad had sold mother's pearl earrings last year. Perhaps it was pert to complain after the pains everyoɩe had been at; Aunt Talmadge was watching her expressionlessly, which meant that there was nothing to be done.

"Once you are Nicholas' wife," she said presently, "he will buy you all you may want, gowns of silk and velvet, and lace and fine shifts, and new hose."

Clemency considered this; it seemed odd to think of Nick buying a girl stockings. She still did not feel that they knew one another; she had had speech with him daily by now and found him no less shy than on the first evening, like a caught wild animal, a deer perhaps; gentle and helpless, ready to quiver with fear at the captor's hand. Without doubt he would make a kind husband, but why would he never meet one's eyes? And why, if he were rich enough to buy so many gowns, had they not

27

obtained him a rich wife? It should have been easy.

But she had asked all these questions already and had only been fobbed off. The only person she had not asked, among the women, was Marguerite Hautboys, whom she did not like. Marguerite had come to Ravensyard for the wedding, leaving her ill-tempered lord and her brood of children at home; and the sight of her beautiful heart-shaped face and dark tresses warmed one, until one looked into her eyes and saw the false glitter there, like a serpent's. Marguerite always spoke smoothly; perhaps she had got in the way of it with Hautboys, who would need such handling; but Clemency did not take to her despite the fact that she was Aunt Talmadge's daughter.

Her mouth drooped; Dad could not leave Court to come to her wedding, he had to ride to Theobalds with the King. She should have known, when he embraced her on parting, that it might be long enough before she saw him again. As for Alice, she was still entirely taken up with pleasuring Savernake, and wrote that she was with child already and could not travel.

So Clemency was alone, in the midst of folk she scarcely knew; and walked to church with the company. She carried a small bunch of pale roses in her hands and had pinned one of them at her breast, below the ruff. At least Marguerite Hautboys was doing her one favour; Dick the lecher was so busy ogling her he had no time to do so to Clemency, which was a blessing. Marguerite looked very fine in crimson velvet which set off her ebony hair and skin of milk. No doubt she outshone the bride.

But now they were at the church, and it was time to stop thinking of Marguerite and remember herself and Nick, and that she would be his wife within moments. Once at the lych-gate John Talmadge gave her his arm, and they went inside and forward to where Nicholas and Penellyn waited, the vows were said and the ring put on Clemency's finger. Coming back up the aisle she saw that a few were in church who had not walked down with them from Ravensyard. She was told that they were neighbours, and given their names. Back at the gate they crowded about her, and there was a comical old man named Sir

Harry Bilbee, who said the rain must not fall on so fair a bride; and a tall man named Sir Bremner Clevelys, who made bold to kiss her so that his grey beard scraped her face, and wished her happy in a voice that might have been her father's. "When all the feasting is done you must visit my wife and me," he said, adding that his wife was abed with a rheum, or she would have come today. "You will be welcome to us both, and Nick also," he said, and the promise warmed her heart a little; at least there were houses to which to go where one would not meet more Talmadges or Hautboys.

A cold wind had begun to blow despite the summer day, and soon they made ready to return to Ravensyard. Clemency walked with her hand on Nick's arm; she had the feeling that he thought of it as fashioned of glass, not flesh. She said little to him; it was wearisome always having to think of something new to say. Back at the house there would be feasting; the cooks, she knew, had been busy since yesterday, and little Theale, Emma's husband, had run about everywhere in his linen cap, making ready.

When she saw the laid table she knew that they had taken much trouble. There was a special dish, a pigeon inside a partridge inside a goose, and there were pasties, and a great side of ham and other meats. Later they brought in a delicate conceit of spun sugar which Theale had made, and there was wine both red and white, and almonds in a bowl, and sweets. Clemency was hungry after the walk to church and back, and ate heartily. At one time she glanced at Nick, who was toying with his food as he always did; small wonder he looked so thin and pale.

"Do you mislike the conceit, husband?" It was strange to use the word, and stranger still that she should use it to Nick; she did not feel truly married. She glanced sideways at him. His weak mouth smiled while he gazed down at the damask table-cloth, spread on the floor to catch the crumbs and bones.

"I find such things pretty, that is true." He spoke absently, as if he had returned from far away. She cast about for something else to say and then someone else to whom to talk, but Aunt Talmadge was deep in converse with her daughter, whom she

29

saw seldom, and the rest were intent on what they ate. Everyone seemed silent, and of a sudden Clemency remembered the harp player Penellyn. She turned to Nicholas eagerly. "Husband, may we not dance?"

"The servants are eating their supper, as you can see; let them finish it." It was John Talmadge who spoke, and Clemency noted with anger that once again he had answered for Nicholas, as if her husband were a child or an idiot. "All that will be changed now I am mistress of Ravensyard," she thought. The warm notion increased her desire for some merrymaking, and the wine she had drunk made her bold. She beckoned to the boy who stood nearby with the wine-jug. "Go down to David Penellyn and bid him play for us." John Talmadge should not have everything his own way.

She saw Penellyn's tall figure rise from its place as he went to fetch his harp, and noted Talmadge's pursed mouth. I have won the first encounter, she thought. She felt her cheeks grow hot with triumph and with wine.

Penellyn played, a succession of sweeping airs from the Welsh hills, sad and plaintive. "Give us some cheer, fellow; play a rigaudon," Dick Talmadge called from where he sat by his mother. He clapped his hands and when the music began again, suddenly led out Marguerite to dance. Her dark hair was too rich to need a frame, and was piled on her head and bound with bands of silver. They twirled about the floor, tall Dick and the dark lovely woman who came up to his shoulder; Clemency could not look at Nicholas for shame. By rights he and she should have been first on the floor, but he had not asked her. After what seemed a long time the gay music stopped, and the breathless pair returned to their places, Marguerite smiling like a cat that has lapped cream. It was no doubt pleasant, at her age—she must be nearing thirty—and in the absence of her lord, to have a personable young man take heed of her. Yet after they had sat down there remained small goodwill about the meal, no laughter or chaffing as is usual at a wedding. Nobody else went out to dance. Clemency saw Dame Joan sit proud and still, and tried to copy her; no one must know that she was hurt by Nicholas' lack of manners and the small deference shown to her as a bride. In future . . . "I will gather the reins in my own hands, and there shall be laughter and friendly faces in this hall. I may be young, but I'm no fool," she told herself. There was some matter amiss with this marriage; very well, she would put it right.

This was difficult.

Later, while the company still ate and drank, she was led to the bride-chamber, Aunt Talmadge and Marguerite assisting her; Dame Joan stayed where she was, among the men. Clemency began to fear she would break into trembling, and before the hated Marguerite; what did she know of marriage? Aunt Talmadge had spoken briefly to her of duty, and she had remembered the alley-cat affairs at Court and been afraid. But she would not ask more of either woman who was with her. Aunt Talmadge herself had lain in two marriage-beds "and small good she got of it, except that she bore Marguerite." But Marguerite herself was the last person to ask.

"There, now you are ready." They had combed out Clemency's silver-fair hair and had set a wreath upon it made of rosemary and heartsease, for quick conception of a child. Then they withdrew to the back of the room while she sat up between the sheets and waited for Nicholas. Shortly he was brought in by John Talmadge, Ralph and Dick, who at once made to rumple the bride where she lay. Clemency set her small teeth in his hand; he withdrew it with a curse.

"The vixen hath made me bleed," he protested. "May you be well pricked in your turn this night, cousin; though I doubt it," he added in a low voice.

The company had come crowding in; it was uncertain how many had seen and heard. Clemency added another stone to her edifice of hate; of them all, she was thinking, Dick Talmadge was the most loathsome. Nicholas, shrinking, was put between the sheets at her side; he looked miserable, and suddenly impatience and anger overtook her; was she so ugly, after all?

31

Presently, after the stocking filled with salt was flung, they were left alone. He said nothing and did not move; she became aware that he was trembling, as she had feared to do. Her anger fled, leaving her with compassion; he was shy and a virgin, like herself. She moved closer and put her arms round him. "Come, lie down," she whispered, "you are cold and I will warm you. Take no heed of their jests." The rest had lurched back to the hall now, where they would be swilling the remainder of the wine. She felt that she was cozening a child; it was no worse than that; strange to think that Nicholas was older than herself by eight years.

His trembling increased and she tried to soothe him with caresses, stroking his body; the spasms now were violent, enough to shake the bed. Yet he did not perform the marriage act. "Never fret, Nick," she murmured gently. "They say these things come in time; there's no haste. Sleep if you will."

"I—I cannot—cannot—" Suddenly she was aware that there was foam between his lips. His shaking increased so that he shuddered away from her, and rolled at last from the bed to the floor, lying there writhing. Clemency slid from the bed and ran round to him; he was lying in a fit, with blood among the foam from his bitten tongue. She pulled at the sheet and tried to insert it between his teeth; they were gripped fast. She began to be afraid, so much so that she did not feel strangeness at the sight of his thin young body, lying naked on the floor. She began to call for help, the more loudly in that no one came at once. They would all be at their carousing, and hearing her cry would think that it was her maidenhead being ravished. Yet someone must come.

The door opened and David Penellyn stood there an instant; then he hurried to the kneeling girl and the prone man. He took Nicholas in his arms and began to talk to him in rapid Welsh. Presently the spasm eased. Nicholas' lips fell apart and with that, a dribble of blood and foam dropped on Clemency's thigh. She remembered that she was naked in front of a servant and, scarlet-faced, shook forward her hair to cover her breasts. Presently, when Nick was calm, Penellyn lifted him back into bed and later flung Clemency her bed-gown. His dark eyes were full of anger.

"I knew it would come to this if they forced him; that is why I kept watch. He must sleep in his bed this night, but you shall not; go to the truckle-bed in the little closet, and sleep there." He had begun to strip covers from the bride-bed, bundling them up in his arms prior to taking them to the further room. Clemency shivered despite the summer heat. "Am I to take your orders?" she asked, safe in the bedgown.

"Someone is to give orders if my master is not to die. Forget that you are the mistress and I a servant and show compassion." The Welsh accent was still pronounced although he spoke now in her own tongue. She regained dignity and, head high, walked barefoot through to the truckle-bed in the little chamber.

"And when they come in the morning, what am I to say?" she called back.

"Say nothing and let them think what they like. You can fool them; you have enough wit."

She obeyed him, crawling at last between the hastily disposed covers of the narrow bed. Penellyn slept with Nick, to ensure his safety.

He was gone by the morning. Later, eyeing one another warily like two she-cats, Dame Joan came with Elizabeth to examine the bride-sheets. They found blood on them and looked at one another coldly. It might mean that the marriage had been consummated; but Nick had a bitten tongue. Questioning the bride later brought no satisfaction; Clemency would tell them nothing.

FOUR

She had to contend with more than the older women and their prying; that very day, John Talmadge sent for her.

She found him in his office, for besides being Nicholas' guardian he had for years done the work of stewarding the great house, keeping a firm eye on all its outgoings. Why was he so devoted? she asked herself. It had not meant riches for him; doubtless power meant more.

He greeted her courteously and drew out a chair. She saw his cold blue glance—how many pairs of chilly blue eyes there were among these Talmadges!—assessing her, and hoped that there would not be further questioning about the marriage-night. She felt weary after the broken sleep in the truckle-bed, from which Emma had wakened her this morning without comment. No doubt the sister knew everything from her brother. Clemency had been dressed in her green gown by the time the women came; wearily, she glanced down at it now, aware of its limp appearance, and saw John Talmadge do the same.

"We must take you into the town this very week to buy new stuffs and satins," he said. "You will find our Wednesday fair comparable with the finest shops in London. My sister will gladly go with you; her judgement is good." He sat back in his chair. "Before then, I wanted to speak with you; there was no leisure earlier."

I have been here for some days now, she thought; he could have found leisure. "You were chosen for Nick," he said, "because your aunt wrote to me that you had wit and courage as well as beauty, and could hold your own in most disputes. The state of affairs here will tax all of your understanding, apart from Nick himself whom you have sworn to love and honour."

"I had sooner sworn after I had been told all this, my uncle."

"No matter. My good-sister Joan—well, you have met her and her sons. They are the danger."

Clemency found her tongue and spoke. "What manner of danger, good uncle? You have but now said that Dame Joan will accompany me to the booths. Yet she does not like me, as I could tell."

"She would like no bride of Nick's."

"Then why was she at the wedding, and here at other times? The house is seldom free of her."

"She hath come to look upon the house as her own and that of her sons. I think that you should hear the tale of Nick's parentage, and about the father of Dick and Ralph. I know you can keep a close tongue in your head." His eyes warmed to a twinkle. "Last night you acted wisely at the feasting when Dick Talmadge led out the dance with . . . my stepdaughter."

"Marguerite is beautiful, and dances well."

"What says that to anything?" he asked irritably. "God He knoweth that I of all men have had leisure to know Marguerite Hautboys. She wrought much harm between her mother and me. But that is not what I wished to speak of. Long since, I and my brother, Nick's father, and our cousin, Joscelyn Talmadge who married my sister Joan, served together under arms for the Queen. Nick—his son is named for him—and I were ever close. Our cousin Joscelyn we did not like. He was a great cunning twisting, blustering fellow, who let nothing stand in the way of his will. He made a good soldier, therefore, in command, but he

36

would have no man order him."

"I understand, my uncle." She could picture the resemblance between Joscelyn's sons and their father. Added to that was the ambition of the woman he had married.

"You and Joscelyn Talmadge both wed cousins," she said hesitantly. It would be impossible for any outsider to judge these Talmadges truly; their clan-pride was close-knit and fierce.

"That is so, and maybe my marriage was barren by reason of it," said John. "But Nick was never a ladies' man and would neither dally nor wed, until when we were on the Scottish border on some business for the Queen, he met a woman of the Armstrongs. Have you heard of that clan?"

"I believe that I have, in stories of the wars."

"They are loyal neither to one side nor the other. She was, as they have it, fey, which is to say mad. The Armstrongs consider themselves descended from a fairy and a bear; an unchancy mating."

"Was she beautiful, Nick's mother?" Clemency felt as if a hand had clutched at her heart. Fey, fairy; it accounted for much.

"Beautiful and half crazed as well. She sowed naught but dissension among us from the beginning of that marriage; we were never friends again. By the mercy of God her son was born before Nick's death, so that he knew he had an heir of his own; he charged me with his guardianship."

Clemency glanced down at her hands, lying cool and white in her lap. Perhaps Nick's fits had come from his crazy mother, but she dared not ask. What kind of bridal had they made for her and Nick, Aunt Talmadge and her husband John between them? If it were not for the house, she thought, I had best return to London.

She said aloud "What became of Nick's mother?"

"The faithless bitch could not even mourn her dead, but married again within the year."

"Is she alive still?"

"After a fashion, but insane. She is kept close in a house in

37

the country."

And they ask me to bear the fruit of it, thought Clemency. She raised her head and looked John Talmadge full in the eyes and said "Have you a likeness of her?"

"The only likeness was buried with Nick. But here—" he drew aside a curtain which hung by the wall—"is a likeness of Nicholas Talmadge the elder, as I knew him."

The likeness was in profile, showing the half-ruff tilted up at the back of the narrow, close-shaven head. Men wore their hair longer nowadays. Nicholas Talmadge had a cold face, she thought. Perhaps his fey bride had wished him dead and had been glad to bestow her beauty where else she might. Insane, and kept close in a house in the country . . .

"What do you want of me?" she said, as he replaced the curtain over Nicholas Talmadge's face. "Why did you send for me today?"

He turned and scanned her. "To show you of what import a son for young Nick may be; to urge you to bear one soon, to keep Dame Joan and her sons from the inheritance. It was well for young Nick to marry, for some accident might have befallen him for all my watchfulness, and still may; they are ever about the house, watching and waiting."

"Can you not keep them out?"

"All hath been courtesy till now; and they would waylay him outside, maybe on his way to church, for he goeth otherwise not much abroad. They would plan a mishap to seem like chance. I thought best—I have always thought so—to have them under my eye, that I might watch them and know when they mean ill."

"You cannot be watchful night and day, uncle."

"For Nick's son I can; and now I have you to aid me, Clemency Talmadge. I am glad that we have had this talk together."

She left him. He had not mentioned, perhaps would never mention, the falling-sickness Nick suffered; he and she would pretend to one another that it was not so.

Her life soon began to set itself into a strange pattern; each night she was undressed by the maid Emma as if to share Nick's bed, and sometimes she would talk with him when he came there; but always before the night was far spent David Penellyn waited, to take the place she should have kept by Nick's side, while she herself made her way to the truckle bed in the closet adjoining. Since John Talmadge's talk with her no one asked about the progress of the marriage, nor did there seem much to question; by day she and Nick were good friends, and he showed her his dog and his raven, and one day his library, which had some books rare even in London. The herbal in it she asked Nick if she might brrow. "Gladly", he said. Thereafter she read of herbs and cures and ills; winter cinnamon for worms, marshmallow and cranesbill for nose-bleeds, infusion of barley for fevers, corncockle for dropsy, lily of the valley to cause nightingales to mate and also to help the heart. Reading whiled away the rainy hours, and when it was fine she walked, for although Nicholas had promised to buy her a half-Arab to mount there was nothing in the stables yet but one old gelding. She walked about the spinney and the cottages and the nearer paths; further into the wood one might lose oneself. She would have liked Nick to accompany her, but he disliked going out; she could understand now how he might fear falling where all could see him. There seemed no herb to cure his ill.

The pony came in due course, and nothing else was denied her. After Aunt Talmadge returned to London Dame Joan came as arranged to Ravensyard, and together they rode into town. There was little talk between them on the way, and Clemency could understand why many feared this fair ageing woman with the proud closed face and shabby clothes. But when she saw the booths with their bales of coloured stuffs for sale she forgot Joan, and delightedly watched while vendors spread out velvets from Genoa with their gentle sheen, figured satins for fine occasions, bright silks for summer. She fingered the lawn, delicate as a cobweb, which they sold her for shifts, promising to put some fine stitching in for herself; the sempstress need not make everything. There was a stand with a wooden head on it to show off ruffs; full, or folded back as the new fashion was so that there was a deep V, which made for comfort. There were staymakers and milliners, the latter showing their wares of tiny feather-trimmed French hats or the new high-crowned ones, such as the Queen liked to set on her frizzed blonde hair. Glovemakers waited in their close tent where the smell of tanned leather clung; Clemency bought four pairs for herself and one pair for Joan, which the lady received haughtily.

"I am not without gear," she remarked unpleasantly. Clemency flushed, taken aback that her gift should be resented. It had been thoughtless, perhaps; but she had meant no harm. How careful one must be with these Talmadges! They were like cats with their claws concealed, then in a moment, out they sprang. She would know better in future than to offer gifts to Joan.

An unpleasant thing happened, not long after the gloves had been exchanged. One tent was full of a noisy crowd, and behind it she could see the Egyptians' camp; they often came where there was spending of money, for they would tell fortunes for silver. The smoke from their fire bade fair to blacken the dainty ruffs in yellow or white on their stands. Clemency wanted to match a piece of lace in daylight against her gown; she went a little way back from the crowd, and suddenly a hand, smelling of sweat and dirt, was put over her mouth. Clemency twisted nimbly, brought up a knee and caught the assailant in the groin. The hand was dropped with a curse, and she saw a man slip like a shadow back towards the camp-fire, where he disappeared among his ragged clan. There was no watch set near; nobody could have helped her if . . . For some reason she could not yet explain to herself, she said nothing to Dame Joan about the incident, nor, on return, to John Talmadge. The same lack of reason caused her, that night, to tell Penellyn, cautioning him not to speak of it to Nick. Looking back it seemed to her that that confidence marked the end of their relations as mistress and servant; but at the time she did not note it.

"I would not be enough of a fool to speak of it to him," he

replied tersely. "But you should be guarded, mistress, when you ride out. Always take a servant in future."

"They are too far away from here to try again. Why would they do such a thing?"

"To ask for money for ransom you, maybe, or it might be also that Dame Joan had a hand in it; she knew where you would be today, close by her in the booths."

"If that is so she hath wasted her silver. I am glad I did not speak of it to her; it must have irked her sorely not to hear anything at all of it on the road back home."

"You are brave enough," he said in a low voice.

When the new clothes were made Clemency felt also fine enough to entertain and to meet her neighbours. In the course of the next few months she went many times to their houses, but always alone or with a servant, as Penellyn had advised. Nick would not venture beyond the wall except to church, and knowing the cause of it now she did not judge him. But the most frequent visitors were still Dame Joan and her sons. They rode over twice weekly to sup, although as yet there had been no return of hospitality; in any case Clemency did not greatly care to see the inside of Marshalhall. It was true that Dame Joan's purse was slender, lacking the inheritance, and in the ordinary way Clemency would not have grudged bite and sup to a woman poorer than herself. But Joan's pride and haughtiness continued unchanged; one never made a friend of her, and no doubt the marred plan at the booths gave her pause for thought. The cold eyes took in everything, and every word exchanged between Clemency and Nick was noted. She did not know whether it were more merciful to Nick to fall silent, or to talk as usual. Dame Joan did not as yet know the truth about the marriage, that was certain "and she shall not find out from me," thought Clemency.

Penellyn always played for them after dinner now; it was one of the changes she had been able to make, to render life more cheerful. Music soothed poor Nick and even made him able to rest easily beside her; sometimes his fingers beat time to the melody pouring from Penellyn's strings. But he never attempted to dance, and Clemency had given it up for herself; there was no heart in it.

FIVE

Watchful as she had begun to be, the next attempt took her unawares; and she had had what could have passed as a warning. One day Penellyn had come to her, his dark eyes rueful.

"Mistress, I cannot play any more till the winter kill. I have broken a string."

She said "But surely you have more to spare?" She knew little of lute-playing, but knew every player kept string-lengths of sheeps' intestines by him.

"I had a roll of sheep-gut which I make myself each year, but it is missing. I cannot replace it now till the saltings in November."

"May such things not be bought in the town? I will give you the money." For John Talmadge was generous with her pin-money, and she had little here on which to spend it. In the booths, which she had not revisited because the fearful remembrance of the gipsy was still strong, they sold everything, ribbons, kerchiefs, essences, oranges, as well as cloth. Surely somewhere there would be music-makers' gear? But Penellyn shook his head.

"I would not have troubled you did they sell it, but they do not; I tried when I last rode into town for Master John."

"Then I am sorry you can no longer beguile our evenings," she said, smiling at him. How deep and fierce his glance was, so different from the cold English gaze! She no longer resented it. It was strange how Welsh blood persisted; no doubt his playing and singing were had from some ancestor in that magical, stubborn country.

She thought no more of the matter, and the days passed and she was busied sewing her clothes with the women. Nick spent all day in his library; she had returned the herbal, had planted herbs, and would know what to do if by chance anyone in the house were sick and they could not find a physician. Suddenly, as if in answer, she heard a man's voice cry out from the narrow stair that led to John Talmadge's office. She ran out of the hall and up to him. He was lying sprawled down the stone steps, his limbs strangely twisted; but he still breathed. Clemency called, and the servants came running, and got Master John to bed; but she suspected that no herb could cure him, and sent for a doctor without delay. When he came, he spoke with her.

"He will not leave his bed again," he said.

"Will he die of the fall?" She could not understand what had befallen shrewd, cold Master John, who descended the steps every day of his life; how had such a thing happened? But the physician was more greatly concerned with the patient than with the cause.

"I do not think that he will die, or not yet. He may live long enough, but he hath taken a blow on his skull and it may affect his wits, his limbs, perhaps both." He gave her instructions as to how Master John was to be fed, like a little child with a cup and spoon; she showed a servant how to do it, later. Then she climbed the stairs to the estate-office slowly, staring down at the worn treads.

If she had not been looking almost absently, she would have found nothing. As it was, could a tiny fragment of curled brown gut have meaning? She knelt down and took it in her hands, staring closely at the stairs and wall. When one looked hard

44

enough it was possible to see two tiny holes in the wood where nails had been placed. Had a string of purloined gut been stretched where John Talmadge, Nicholas, herself or anyone unknowing might trip and fall? It was one answer. She sent for Penellyn in a kind of panic; he was out of doors, and by the time they found him it was growing dark, and they had to go over the place together by the light of a tallow dip. But he saw the holes, and nodded.

"It hath been done. Someone commonly in the house hath done it."

"But who could have done such a thing? One of the servants?"

"Maybe, if he were paid. I will keep sharp watch. While the physician was here and you with him, whoever it was would have had time to come and remove the nails and gut. But it was brittle and broke, and he did not note that. Mistress, have a care to yourself."

"I will, I will. Tell me at once of any strange matter you find, any thing that should not be."

He promised, bowed, and went. Left kneeling there she realised that now John Talmadge was bedridden and afflicted, there was no steward at Ravensyard. She went into the office and examined the books. They had been well and honestly kept, clearly written in a neat and clerkly hand. The following day she sent for Penellyn again.

"Can you write?"

The dark brows drew together. "I can do so. I have had some education. When Master Nicholas was a child I shared his tutor, to be company to him. Master John allowed it." He stood proudly, almost as if she had insulted him by the question. Impulsively, Clemency laid a hand on his arm.

"I should like you to become my steward at Ravensyard. You shall have the full wage that was taken by Master John, and I will examine the books once a month." Ravensyard, as she had found by reading John's entries, was a rich appanage, more so than she had dreamed, with the rents from farms and cottages, and other monies invested by John. It was no mean task that she had appointed to Penellyn.

He bowed in the way he had, as though it were an honour and not servitude he undertook. "I accept the task gladly," he told her. "I would aid you in every way I can."

She dismissed him then; she was inclined to forget that he was, after all, a servant.

Aunt Talmadge hurried to Ravensyard from town on hearing of John's fall, but on being led to his bedside she seemed to accept with equanimity the fact that there was nothing she could do for him. In fact she spent less time with him than with Clemency or, later, her own daughter Marguerite. "Marguerite will not ride over to see her stepfather; she says the children are sickening with a fever, and she must keep close to the house." But as the days passed and the fever must have waned Aunt Talmadge began to visit Hautboys, sometimes for two or three days together. However she seemed no longer to regard Marguerite as being of her flesh; she always spoke of her with reverence, as though they were strangers chance met. There was some bar to the mother's feeling for her daughter; could it be the presence of Hautboys? Or was it that Marguerite herself cared for nothing but her own beauty and even regarded the children as reflections of it? No one knew, and it was not a matter Clemency could discuss with anybody at Ravensyard. She herself persisted in the uprush of dislike she felt whenever Marguerite's name was mentioned, but could not have told why.

So John Talmadge lay silent and alone, except for the servant who sat by him and for Nick and Clemency's daily visits. In time Aunt Talmadge went back to London. She wrote to Clemency on return, enclosing a note from poor Alice; Alice had miscarried, Gregory Savernake had some ill humour in his chest, and the physician's fees were high. Could Clemency lend her twenty pounds? Clemency sent that and more, knowing she would not see a penny of it again. The world at large seemed troubled and ill; the King had some strange sickness and they had to plunge him into hot baths, which was a good thing as he never washed himself; and as for Dad, he never wrote nowadays. Perhaps some lady was paying him court again. But one thing came to cheer Clemency; the little half-Arab mare.

She liked to ride and had told Nicholas so in one of their first talks together. To her joy, on her first birthday at Ravensyard he showed her that he had not forgotten; he led her down to the stables and there stood the little cream-coloured pony, her mane and tail groomed and her coat in bloom with health, and a saddle of scarlet cloth ready waiting. Clemency gave a cry of pleasure and ran to the mare, running her hands over the proudly arched neck, the velvet nose. Then she ran back to kiss Nicholas and thank him for his gift. He accepted the kiss awkwardly, his face red and his eyes on the ground. Clemency laid her arms about his neck.

"May I not thank you?"

"Ay."

"It is kind in you; she is all I wanted. You are so good to me that I wish I could bring you joy."

He answered slowly "It gives me joy to look upon you, you are so beautiful," speaking in a low voice so that the grooms might not hear. Tears came into her eyes and, paying no more attention to the mare for the time, she persuaded Nicholas to come and look at her herb-garden, where some of the seeds had sprouted. Then he took her to his library and they read awhile together; but the sun was shining, and she knew impatience to be on the mare's back, seated in the scarlet saddle, trying her paces. That afternoon she contrived it; and came back with her cheeks stung rosy by the wind. "It were a fair ride, mistress?" enquired the head groom. "Glad I am to see a good beast in the stables again at Ravensyard. Thou'rt not afeared to go alone? I'd ha' come with thee, had thou bade me."

"Naught can happen here. Next time I mean to ride to visit Lady Clevelys; maybe tomorrow."

She rode to Clevelys, and on the way made herself familiar with the further reaches of the estate; the cottagers ran out, stopping what they were at to watch the fair young mistress of Ravensyard pass by in the saddle. A pity so handsome a wench were matched with that girl-man, said some; but others remembered Master Nick only for his gentleness and charity.

Margery Clevelys was weeding her garden, and after taking Clemency indoors for wine she asked her if she would like to take home cuttings. Clemency was pleased; there was a full acre of garden, far larger than her own at Ravensyard. "Alack, we have no child," said Margery, "so I pass my time while my lord is absent in learning of herbs, and growing them."

They discussed herbs fit for cookery and poultices, and Clemency admired the knot-garden just coming into tiny flower. Her own piece of rough ground was not yet in any way like this, but she hoped for much with the years. "One must have patience with a garden," said Margery. Her own face was plain and kind, seamed with wistfulness; she seemed lonely except for her lord, and Clemency welcomed her as a friend. She rode home with rootlings wrapped in linen to keep them moist, and when she reached the house set them in water at once. She would plant them tomorrow.

SIX

Nick's pet raven was tame enough to take crumbs from Clemency's hand. It was often to be found near the upper turret on a ledge there, beyond the narrow window. One day she had mounted the twisting stairs and was feeding it; she did not hear steps behind her.

"That bird would as soon peck out your eyes as take bread; they like carrion."

She spun about, hearing the bird flap off as if maligned; and saw Ralph Talmadge standing below her, a narrow smile on his lips. Clemency drew herself up.

"They did not tell me you had come to the house," she said coldly.

"No, why should they? It has been our custom to stop here freely during my lifetime, and my brother's. Are things to be altered now? Are you so set on being mistress here? You may contrive it with poor Nick as he is; you will cozen him as readily as his raven doth."

"You will not speak to me of my husband thus. In future I shall tell the servants to inform me when you or your kin ride here. That is plain courtesy."

49

"I can see you know little of Ravensyard, despite your probings," he said, smiling secretly. Ralph had a curious effect on her; she did not dislike him as she did his brother, but could not admire him and doubted if any woman could love him. But that was for others to say.

"Tell me what I do not know," she said suddenly, unwilling to be at enmity.

"Why, since we are here, I will tell you of the Tredesc couple."

"Did they live here?" Her brow wrinkled; she had not heard the name before; was it of these parts?

"Perforce, and not for long. Mary Tredesc had been an heiress whom the lord of Ravensyard in those days desired to marry, but she was given to Simon Tredesc and loved him well. One day they were riding between towns when the lord of Ravensyard captured them, and had them brought prisoner to the house. He placed Simon in the dungeon and held Mary at his will, it may have been in this very room. He made her pleasure him before he would send Simon any food. Time and again it happened, and soon enough she was with child by my lord. She was made to bear the child and then, the lord having tired of her, she was thrown into the dungeon with her husband, and they both starved to death. Her ghost is said to walk here, wailing and wringing hands."

"A cruel story. How long ago was that?"

"Maybe from the time of King Stephen, or perhaps King John. Many cruel deeds were done then, there being no law and order to prevent them."

Clemency shuddered. "I would wish you had not told me, except that I like to know all I may of Ravensyard."

"Meseemed as much, which is why I told you the tale. You have courage enough to hear of unpleasing matters without fainting, as fools do. Indeed I think you have the heart of a man in that fair breast. My brother Dick admires the outer part, and I the inner."

"And your mother?" She did not comment on the matter of Dick, who ogled every woman.

50

Ralph trailed his finger along the sill. "She has the heart of a man also, which makes her your enemy. If the two of you ever come to arms, I tremble for the outcome."

"I do not believe that anything would make you tremble, Ralph. You have your own courage."

"Maybe I have not been tried," he said, and turned away. She followed him down the staircase and when it came to the narrow hall entry, he stood aside to let her pass. A cheerful fire burned in the hall; they might have been in a different house from the one that held Mary Tredesc's ghost, and her sad story.

The days passed, and nothing of note happened except the death of the parson who had married Clemency and Nick. This was not unexpected, as for a long time he had had a great belly on him, like a woman about to give birth; one night after evensong he had begun to scream with pain, and his innards burst and he died. He would not be much missed, for he had been too ill to visit much or to preach fine sermons. Nobody wept for him at the funeral except his young niece, who was an orphan and did not know where she was to go.

SEVEN

Clemency was returning home by the familiar path from Clevelys. It had been pleasant there as always, with laughter and friendly cheer. This was always so, whether she visited Bremner and Margery or they came to Ravensyard. Today Margery had ordered sweetmeats and hippocras to be sent up and they had all laughed together, banishing Margery's habitual melancholy. Sir Bremner could be like a boy when he chose. What a pity Nick would never ride over with her! The company would do him all the good in the world.

She had done what she could in making Ravensyard a cheerful place over the winter; several of the neighbouring families had ridden over to dine and sleep. It had been pleasant to watch Nick's guarded face break into smiles and even laughter; he had been kept too close by John Talmadge. Yet there were still times when Nick seemed remote from her and the whole world, and he had not yet made her a wife. She put such thoughts behind her as she cantered the little mare home. This freedom to be in her own company was one she enjoyed also; she hardly ever took a groom.

The path led straight through the thinning coppice of trees

beyond the great wood. In autumn and winter one could see Ravensyard turrets rise beyond. She slipped out of the saddle and let the mare walk; it was early yet, she had made good speed from Clevelys. How pleasant to be alone, free of the wistful brown gaze of Nick or—she faced the truth—David Penellyn and his dark smouldering fires. She reminded herself for the hundredth time that the man was nothing but a servant; why should he cause her disquiet? Yet he did so, and she saw more of him now that he was her steward, carrying out his tasks well.

A man's voice hailed her, breaking the silence. It was Dick Talmadge, mounted on his great grey. She was not pleased to see him and started to remount, but he was down before she reached the stirrup. He slipped her mare's reins into his hand along with those of his own. "The day is fine," he observed. "May we not walk awhile together?"

She said coldly "I must go home; I have been away three hours."

"Then make it four, Clemency; no man's your master."

She resented his speech, but it made no odds; he had flung both sets of reins over a branch, and had in some way compelled her hand to rest on his arm, then taken it in his grasp. He was leading her between the trees. She would have broken away, but suddenly as they came to a brake where last year's bracken and leaves lay, he twisted quickly and flung her down with all the strength of his great body.

"I do not waste time, mistress," she heard him say; and as she struggled to rise he was on top of her. She would have cried out, but he put a hand on her mouth; with the other, he burrowed up her skirts. The clumsy farthingale impeded her movements, and although she fought furiously it was useless. Soon he had her skirts over her head; any crying she might make would not be heard, or not heeded. She felt him lift her by the knees and jerk her legs apart, forcing his body between them. He stuffed the folds of her skirt against her mouth to stifle her outcry; she heard him laugh.

"I knew you were virgin. Cousin Nick is no man. Permit me to solace you, sweetheart."

54

There was no way now in which she could prevent his forcing her. Her hands beat uselessly by her sides among the folds of her dress; by then, he had entered her twisting struggling body. She felt the pain of deflowering, the stiffening of his great member in her untried parts. He was inflamed and eager, and thrust hard. Shortly the blood flowed, soaking her shift.

He rode her without mercy. They might have lain there perhaps a quarter of an hour, her pride now forcing her to keep her bitten lips shut; she could sense the hot flow of his seed in her, feeling his body's rhythm above her own while his weight crushed her too greatly for response. He was laughing.

"You like it well enough, eh? You are not the prim little wench who came so coldly from London last summer. By the name of God, no one in all that city deflowered you, and I have done so; is that not a cause for boasting?"

He clawed her skirts down that he might see her face, but she lay with eyes closed, tears oozing from below the lids. She would not gratify him by speaking or crying out again. Already her mind was forming a plan that would put his to naught.

He was not done with her. From time to time he took his pleasure, not withdrawing till he was sated; his face had grown red and he was breathless, like a man who has ridden far. He was full of triumph and let her know of it.

"If I have got you with child, sweetheart, never fear. I am the heir. We have put a wrong right, have we not? My son by you shall own Ravensyard; so much the better that he is of your blood and mine. I have coveted you since that first day of all when you would not look at me, and I have you now, Clemency, I have you now."

"No." It was the first time she had spoken. The thing of which he talked was so abhorrent that she opened her eyes and answered him, while he still lay within her. "There will never be a son of yours in Ravensyard," she said clearly. "Sooner I would see the place burn about my ears."

He had to punish her for that, and by the time he withdrew from her, leaving her raped, bleeding, exhausted, bruised, he was still certain of triumph. "I do not please women ill," he said smugly. "You are better off with me than with that Welshman you keep about you. Faith, I did not know or not whether he had beaten me in the race. God's will and man's will know no let. One day, sweet, you shall be mine again—" and he thrust his hand down her bodice and tweaked her breast—"for your flesh is not for Nicholas; no woman's is so. He hath no eye for any thing but books, which worms eat. They will eat us one day also, sweetheart; why waste time in coyness, as the poets say?"

Suddenly she took her fingernails and clawed his face, narrowly missing his eyes as he jerked away. He gathered her hands in his one fist and slapped her, measuring it, again and again with the other. She felt her face and ears burn.

"You shall pay for that, my mistress. Do you remember biting me on your wedding night? I wished you well pricked then, but knew it would not happen; this is better." He stretched himself, aware of the pleasure in his own flesh.

"I loathe you," she said. She would never ride forth alone again on the mare. She felt shame that the clean honest animals, tethered nearby, should have witnessed this filth that he had done upon her.

"You will yet learn to like me, for I will have it so."

"You will not. I will have you turned away from Ravensyard; none of your pinchbeck kin shall come there again."

"It shall not be as you say, but as I say," he told her, but it was like a boy's boasting. Even he was tired; presently he bestowed his limp member back in its codpiece. She tore herself from under him, adjusted her dress, and stumbling to where the horses waited took the mare's reins, and walked unsteadily up the path that led to the house. Behind her she could hear his laughter.

She went straight to her room, and called for Emma. When the maid came she found her mistress whey-faced, with her teeth chattering and blood on her shift.

"Fetch me a warm brick to my bed, for I would go there. You may tell them in the house that I have had a miscarriage. I should not have ridden out today in my condition. Make sure they hear of it."

Emma dropped to her knees and cast her arms about the quivering, slender body. "My little mistress, what is it, what wrong hath been done you? Men are beasts."

"Stop that. Do not talk except to say what I have told you. I miscarried after the ride; it is too late to do anything. Put me to bed, then go and tell the house. That is all you need do; I shall contrive."

She dosed herself with smut of rye, pennyroyal, every drug she knew of to procure abortion. It made her ill, but that was part of the tale of the miscarriage. Alice, after all, had miscarried of her child in London last year and had been ill in bed many weeks. Other folks' misfortunes could be fashioned into blessings for oneself . . . that brute . . . she need never see him again, she would be even with him and all of them.

She watched familiar faces come and pass before her bed, saw poor Nick weep without knowing why; she must comfort him. It was likely enough Dick Talmadge had boasted by now of his prowess; she must never move a muscle of her face to show that it was the truth. She need not see Dame Joan, nor any of them. They could do nothing in face of the tale she had spun to explain the blood.

In a few days she was able to be thankful. Her courses had come back; any seed of Dick's was rendered useless in her by the herbs. Never again would she be taken unawares; never again would she ride out alone on the little mare. Solitude was safe only in Ravensyard; and there she would stay.

Meantime she had sent for Penellyn. She received him in bed, eyes enormous in her pale face, shining hair spread on the pillow. She spoke to him, putting out her hand.

"I sent for you," she said, "to tell you that from this day on neither Joan Talmadge nor any of her kin will enter this house. If you find any servant here who is in their pay, dismiss him. Those are all my orders; obey them."

His mouth trembled and she thought he seemed distraught.

57

"Do you understand me?" she said, and he bowed his head.

"I understand. I am your servant," he said, and she knew that she could trust him and that the house would henceforth be free of any of the Talmadge kin, or their minions.

She lay and listened to the ravens' croaking from the roof. When it did not come, there was something uncanny in the silence. Presently she left her bed and went downstairs. She had not, after all, suffered for more than the moments it had taken. The matter would never be mentioned again.

After he had finished his day's work Penellyn took a horse from the stables, well-stocked now as they were, and rode it down to a tavern where Dick Talmadge was wont to spend his evenings. If he were not there tonight, Penellyn would return. But he was fortunate; on entering he could see Dick's golden head, back turned, below the lantern, and hear his loud laughter; although it was still early in the evening he was part drunk already and sat boasting among a crowd of noisy idlers. Penellyn frowned; he would sooner have beaten a sober man.

He went to Dick and tapped him on the shoulder. "I would have a word with you outside, if you please." Dick turned, and gaped a little in astonishment; what was Clemency's Welsh steward doing here? He was a damned unsociable fellow, and in any event a servant; why use him in any other way? "Say what you have to say, and be damned," replied Dick, and the company gaped in its turn; Penellyn's frown deepened till Clemency would hardly have known her deferential bailiff.

"It is a private matter," he said tersely. The company stared for instants, then returned to its noisy talk. They did not care for Dick Talmadge and his affairs were not their concern.

Dick grinned. Could that little she-cat, Clemency, have a message for him? Would she perhaps relish another tumble, for all her protesting to the contrary, and have sent word by this fool? He must find out, to be sure; curiosity overcame his natural idleness, and he rose from his place. Yawning—the inn was hot—he made his way out after Penellyn. When they were alone the Welshman faced him; they were of a height.

"I will thrash you on the road if you will, that all may hear of it; or you may meet your punishment privily in the woods, and then take yourself home."

Dick laughed; the insolence of the fellow amused him. "Why, you Welsh rat, it is you yourself who will receive a sounder thrashing than you've known since you entered service," he said. He launched there and then at Penellyn, who was ready for him and deflected the blow by twisting aside; then he took Dick's arm in a grip that threatened to dislocate the shoulder. As the other yelled in pain and surprise, Penellyn brought his horse-whip from behind his back and cut Dick squarely across the face. The blood ran down into Dick's eyes; he lowered his head like a bull, and charged. The two men began to wrestle, Dick with force and weight, Penellyn with cunning but hampered by the whip he clutched in one fist. In the end, he used foot and hand to throw the big man down and was on him in a flash, using his whip. Soon Dick Talmadge was a grunting, punished wreck; his eyes were blind with blood, and his whole body screamed. The whip hissed down again and again, and Dick writhed in agony. If he might only get his hands on the Welsh rat, for one instant only, to wrest it from him and give as good as he'd been given, or better . . . some day . . .

He had begun sobbing early, as cowards do. He would have to explain to his mother how he came to be as he was, and already he could foresee her cool contempt. Never mind it now . . . the devil . . . ah, if he had breath!

Penellyn whipped the breath, the voice and the swagger out of him. Then he stood over the fallen lump of flesh and said quietly "If you ever lay hands on my mistress again, I will kill you."

Dick was sobbing and did not answer. Presently the blows ceased and he heard Penellyn mount and ride home. If he himself had men to bring . . . He raised his head; there was no one on the road; incredibly, it had all of it happened in the space of minutes. Some of the fellows in the inn might have come. He sobbed again. Better after all if they did not see him; he'd been made to look a fool, a fool . . .

He dragged himself to where his horse was and gingerly got into the saddle and made, carefully, for Marshalhall. No one must know of this except his family, or he would be mocked; to have been thrashed by a servant! Wait till he met Penellyn again. He comforted himself with this reflection during the ride, while his wounds throbbed painfully.

EIGHT

"You should have let well alone. Nicholas is unlikely to give her an heir; in time all would have come to us, without your meddling."

It was she who could not let the matter alone, he thought resentfully. "To us, mother, to *us*? *I* am the heir, and 'tis to me all should come. My sons will inherit; as well beget them now as later. She is a toothsome piece and I had her maidenhead, I swear, in the spinney."

Dick, only part recovered from Penellyn's thrashing four days ago, stretched himself with caution, leaned back in the chair whereon he sat till its carved legs creaked with the weight; poured himself more wine, and drained the cup rapidly. He was still sullenly nourishing his hurts; one day, he swore, that rat of a steward should pay. As for the chit, whom he'd had till he'd emptied himself, and her tale of a miscarriage she'd set about to make naught of it; if he had hold of her again, he'd rape her till she couldn't stand. If only—

"You are drunk, and do not know what you are saying," replied Dame Joan coldly. "It is best in any case if your exploits be not spread abroad. They are not to your credit; your lusts are

61

a byword, and to have ravished Nicholas' wife will do you no good; she is liked hereabouts, and he doth no harm."

"It is she who hath done the harm by marrying Nicholas in the first instance." Dick gave his loud laugh, and refilled his cup, while his mother stared coldly; he had no notion of strait-ened means. "They say his fits have lessened since she came; that may give him a longer life, which suits us ill." He twirled the cup in his fingers, and thought of the wretched servant who he knew Ralph had bribed to set the piece of gut across the stairs; it might hopefully have killed Nick or Clemency, but at least John Talmadge had been put out of the way for his lifetime and no watching, cold eyes would prevent him, Dick, from doing his further will. Yet Clemency was sharp, and now she was an enemy.

Ralph had been sitting silent in the window-bay, examining his nails. He lifted his head and surveyed the occupants of the room with cool hazel eyes. "There is a rider coming," he told them.

"We have servants still; let them bring word of who he is," replied Dame Joan coldly. The room in which she sat with her sons was almost empty of furnishings, and the cold daylight struck on bare walls; even the fire had not been lit in the hearth. Since the death of Joscelyn Talmadge it had been necessary to practise thrift; Joan had made a virtue of necessity, but the thought chafed her pride even while she felt thankful for a good price for her missing tapestries. Were Dick richly endowed, no doubt, he would find a good wife and do less harm with women; but he had nothing to occupy his time and nowhere to go but the taverns. When he had come home bruised and bleeding the other night she had hardly been able to hide her shame. Now, after this latest scandal, they had all best stay away from Ravensyard, at any rate for the meantime; they would not, understandably, be welcome. If Dick or Ralph could but attract a rich bride! There would be sons in plenty then to inherit Ravensyard and the fortune there, even though she herself might not live to see it. She stared down at her long hands, which in her Court days had brought forth many a love-song from infatuated young men. The hands were still beautiful, but their lily smoothness had roughened. The sharp face of the old Queen who had banished her from delight came, gleaming with jewels and with red wig blazing; if it had not been for that, who knew whom she herself might have wed? But it was useless to dwell on the past. Age came, and one could not stay it; pride however stayed, pride of family and of name. She had always been a Talmadge; after her expulsion from Court it had been for this reason rather than from love or convenience that she had married her cousin Joscelyn. She could hardly recall his features now and did not often try; life was the same without him as it had always been, except that she had lacked a protector while the boys were young. Well, when all was said and done she had contrived. Ambition was with her still, and would be until she died. If only Dick would control his follies! Of Ralph she had no complaint.

The rider had come to the door; presently their man-servant came in with a letter, which he handed to Dame Joan. "Madam, the messenger would not wait for an answer."

"Then there is none." She broke the seal, and scanned the contents with the blue eyes whose sight was almost as sharp as ever. Despite the servant's presence she gave an exclamation.

"Bad news, mother?" enquired Ralph idly. He admired his mother in that, unlike most other women, she did not weep or wail at misfortune when it came; nor were there ever unseemly demonstrations of affection or joy; doubtless she was a stranger to the last. Always she sat like a queen, head high, and the sense of power he felt rising in him since the episode of John Talmadge's accident had, he knew, come to him from her.

"Bad news for some, as it may be, but it makes no odds to us. Marguerite Hautboys' husband hath taken a fall while hunting, and his neck is broke. Ralph, you will ride over to the funeral."

"Why Ralph alone, mother?" said Dick pettishly.

"Because Marguerite Hautboys will not need your solacing as soon as she's widowed. Ralph, get the horse saddled while I pen a letter after all; it is discourteous not to. I never liked Hautboys, and his wife is evil. But one of us must go."

"I will go too," pouted Dick, "and console pretty Marguerite for all you say. You fancy evil where none is, mother."

"Not I," said Dame Joan.

Elizabeth Talmadge left London again to be with her daughter Marguerite. Both sat together in their mourning while a scattering of neighbours and near kin came to the church for the burial service. Elizabeth was pleased; most of them she had known for years, and would enjoy meeting them after; it was useless to pretend that any mourned Peter Hautboys, for none did.

Marguerite, her exquisite profile concealed beneath her widow's veil, her feelings placid, nudged her mother and said in an undertone "We are honoured today; Nick hath come with Clemency." They watched the thin, white-faced form shamble down the aisle beside his wife, who led him. He stared at the coffin resting in the aisle with an expression of sorrow which was not feigned. Nick had never disliked anyone, not even the bullying Hautboys. Clemency had persuaded him to come, as they would travel in the litter; she was still afraid of riding out alone, and could share his fears. All she had said was "I should like my husband's company," and he had been persuaded to come, feeling his heart give way as it did whenever he looked at Clemency. How beautiful she was! If only—

But he was not as other men, and knew it. He hated leaving the world that he had made his own; his books, and familiar things; it was as though he feared the very air. Clemency sat close by him through the service, clasping his fingers in her own.

The readings stopped and the parson's voice intoned *Man that is born of woman hath but a short time to live*. The men in the company filed out after the coffin, which six of them bore. "Stay by me," murmured Clemency to her husband. It was not for Nick to go out to the sight of a dug grave and stand alone among mourners. To her anger, Dick Talmadge turned as he passed them, a sneer on his handsome face. It was the first time since the rape that she had set eyes on him, and she felt the colour rise in her cheeks.

"Hiding behind your wife, Nick? Play the man and come out with us all; we seldom have the pleasure of your company." His tone echoed the sneer. Clemency met his eyes, outfacing him.

"My husband will not go with you," she said clearly. Dick laughed in a way that showed he had drunk wine; the church was by now mostly empty, with the women in the porch. "Why," said Dick, "a good husband he is to you, I'll warrant; did you tell him of your miscarriage I heard of? Did she tell you that, Nick? Such a matter cannot be unless the wench hath lain with a man. You must be a husband in truth, though few give you credit."

"Will you go?" said Clemency. She stood confronting the tall broad figure with her own slender height, partly as if to screen Nicholas, partly to show the contempt she felt for this bully and ravisher. "Go, and bury your dead; we will go home."

"My dead? Hardly so, though it leaveth Marguerite a widow, and that pleaseth me. She would be good sport in bed, I'll warrant; more so than yourself, Madam Clemency, with your mim airs to prove yourself chaste, which you are not. Why, see how Nick trembles! I doubt you'll get him back in the litter now; he is sore distraught at being wed to a whore."

"Be silent." She had returned to Nicholas, but he was already shaking as he would do when the fits came upon him. She had no means of knowing whether he understood more than half of what had been said. Desperate, she beckoned to one of the Hautboys' serving-men who had not yet gone, and together they contrived to get Nick, his head turned from them, back into the litter, like a child. "I beg of you to hold me excused to our kin," said Clemency to the man, and gave him a coin from her purse. "Tell Mistress Hautboys that I will write."

The journey home to Ravensyard was unspeakable; Nicholas had such spasms that she thought he was going to die, and at no time would he look at her or answer when she called his name. She knew why; that time she had been ill he had not fully understood the matter; now, he did so.

It was long since he had had his fits; she fetched the same physician to him that attended Master John. She was near tears; would Nick never trust her more? She was fond of him as one might be of a pet animal or child; she would not have hurt him for the world. Yet now—

"His humours are sorely disordered, worse than I have seen in him before," the physician said. "He must rest, and on no account leave the house."

"May he walk in my garden?" He had shown interest in the springing plants and she had been teaching him the names, many of which he had seen in his herbal. Would they never walk there together again? The physician pursed his mouth.

"Not yet, certainly not yet; when he mends a little. Let him have wine mixed with water, and no red meat. If he needs it I will bleed him tomorrow; but mayhap after a night's rest he will be better."

"I hope that he will," said Clemency.

The next few days were sad; Nick improved, but would not speak to her. In the end she left him alone; her presence seemed to do more harm than good, and perhaps, lacking her, he might at least return to what he had once been. She lay on her bed and wept, then sat up and took stock of herself.

There must be an heir. If Nick could never give her one, then—as he thought her unchaste—she would, perhaps, be so, to that end; only for that. It must be someone who had some shadow of claim to Ravensyard; not Dick Talmadge—she shuddered—but some other, some other . . .

Why did she deceive herself? She had known all along who it must be.

She sent for him. He came and stood before her, bowing slightly; in some manner his bow never meant subservience.

Now that he was here she was afraid; what she had to say was unwomanly, and he might judge her so. But it must be said; she raised her eyes.

"Penellyn, you will know I have had the physician to my

husband. There is little hope that . . . There is an ill humour in the brain, he says." She was talking wildly. "It may never cure; nor will he ever give me an heir. It is my duty to make one for Ravensyard. I—I know well that you will keep silent on it."

"I will keep so," said Penellyn. He stood without moving, as though he knew what more she had to say. She looked down at her fingers and twined them together; then her eyes met his own again.

"It is part of it hate. I will not have that woman and her sons inherit."

She folded her hands resolutely over one another. "You are of the old blood here," she said clearly. "If a son of yours and mine were to have the house pass to him, it would not be so great a fault."

"I will give you a son."

The words were said with quiet confidence and trust, without pretended delay in assessing her meaning, or any boastfulness. Then he bowed and was gone. She sat on, feeling a kind of lightness invade her heavy heart. For the first time in long there seemed to be hope for the future, hope for herself, even, in a way, for Nicholas. It would not be so wicked, she told herself again. Penellyn's forebears had owned Ravensyard from time immemorial; their blood had soaked the stones.

That night he came to her, in the great bed she had already had moved from an upper chamber to replace the truckle-bed on which she had formerly had to lie. There was a quarter-moon, and by it she saw the whiteness of his shirt, and heard his breathing. He did not speak and might have been a ghost, a visitant. But he was flesh and blood; he came to the bed and slid into it and lay with her. From the beginning she was conscious of the difference between his handling of her and Dick's rough raping; she had not known a man could be so gentle. He used her, she thought, as though she were a princess and he a god; presently she wanted to cry out in ecstasy, but dared not lest any hear. Instead, she hid her face against his shoulder.

Afterwards he left as quietly as he had come, and she slept.

When she awoke it was broad day, and she wondered if it had been a dream that he had come to her. Later that day when she saw him his manner had not changed and was as always. They spoke only of household matters.

Again when it was night he came, and each night that week and the one after. By now her flesh had begun to acquire the bloom of a loved woman; looking in her mirror she could see herself younger, calmer, somewhat like the girl who had first come here from London, but sleek and content, with the strain of worry almost gone from her face and eyes. She tried to make herself think not of Penellyn, but of the coming heir. That, not the nights during which he must be conceived, was her concern. For she would conceive, she was certain; she felt at once soft as velvet and hard as iron.

After the third week she felt queasy in the morning, and was sick into the privy. Emma Theale was about the room setting out her gown for the day; she busied herself about the bed-chest with Clemency's shifts and hose, and shook out the folds of the gown and brought out a newly-laundered ruff of lawn and point lace. Presently she dressed Clemency and their talk was as usual between maid and mistress; there might have been nothing for Emma to note in the latter's pallor and heavy eyes. But that night Penellyn did not come to Clemency, nor on any night thereafter.

NINE

Dick Talmadge had flung himself down by a woodland stream after a long ride which left his horse steaming. He was in a black temper and could see no way in which he might redeem himself. His mother—he admitted he was weak against her—had betrothed him to the daughter of a squire two counties away in the Midlands; he had seen the girl once, and she did not attract him. She was fifteen and had a solid dowry "and so," he thought, "she must be plain." One could not expect good fortune to drop all things into one's hand. Margaret Norreys was a stout little person and at her age, not uncommonly, had blotches on her face. He could not fancy the marriage and yet must make it; the family's estate was at a low ebb. Could not Ralph marry her? he had asked, and his mother had looked at him with her blue stare, and the vestiges of a smile.

"What, Dick, you who were the heir to the Ravensyard fortune and all its acres? What should cozen Norreys' silver but that promise? Ralph hath naught to offer but a younger brother's part."

So Dick, fuming, had had to let the arrangements stand; he was to be married in the autumn. But now it was summer, with every green leaf spreading to the sun; here in the wood it was cool. He blinked his angry eyes open and beheld the vision of an angel; an angel and a large dog.

She was wrapped in veils, the alaunt by her on a lead; it looked fierce. Her walk and her figure were exquisite. Who was she? He must enquire. He sat up from his petulant couch and brushed down his tunic with his hands; he would ask her the way, that was it; he was lost.

She had already seen him, and stopped in her tracks. Dick stumbled to his feet, grinning and uncertain. "Fair lady, can you tell me the way I must take to Marshalhall?"

"And a bigger rascal never asked me, for you know the way well. Out upon you, Dick! We danced together at Ravensyard, before I was widowed."

"Mistress Hautboys!" He felt like a great fool, as she no doubt thought him. "Forgive me, I did not know you veiled," he said; and would sooner, he was thinking, know you unclad. She laughed. "I do but protect my name from wanton tongues, so soon after my husband's death," she said provocatively. "A widow is expected to sit mourning for many months, and truth to tell I had a desire to walk in the cool woods, out of the sun."

She unwound her veil, letting it lie about her shoulders, and he could see her lily-flower skin, red mouth and dark rich hair. "Mistress, our desires match," he said. "May I escort you?" He did not look down at the alaunt, which was straining at its leash. Marguerite stroked its head, and it was quiet. As well I brought it, she was thinking; he hath a name for throwing women in the moss.

They walked together, and spoke of he knew not what; he was enthralled by her body and her grace, and by the fact that she was now free of Peter Hautboys, rot the fellow's soul. Who would have thought that she was the mother of sons? She was slim as a girl, except that her bosom was full and her flesh had the blossoming of maturity. Desire took him and made his mouth dry.

He was forced to contain himself by the alaunt's presence. At the end of their walk, Marguerite did not bid him return to the house with her, but said farewell gracefully, winding her veil once more about her face. "When may we alk again together?" he asked, blushing like a boy. Behind the veil he saw her smile.

"But I hear that you are betrothed, Dick; why do you not walk with your affianced bride?"

Everything she said pricked him to desire. He began to bluster; he was damned if he would marry Margaret Norreys now, or any other since this dazzling vision had come to him. It was as if he had never seen her before, although they had danced . . . when was it, at Ravensyard?

"Mistress," he swore, "I will have no bride but you."

"Oh, fie, Dick Talmadge. I am old enough to be . . . your elder sister." She was enjoying this flirtatious talk with a man younger than herself, who so evidently thought her desirable. Plans ran swiftly through her mind; there might be no money now, but in time, folk said, when Nick Talmadge died in one of his fits, this boy would be heir to Ravensyard and its fortune. It might be better than nothing—and who else would wed a penniless widow?—to encourage his attentions; but there must be marriage at the end of them. She had no wish to be any man's wanton, but she would relish this big golden creature in her bed after Hautboys, who had been inept and mean.

She smiled, cutting short Dick's renewed protestations, and gave him her promise to walk again in the woods if it were fine; not tomorrow, nor the day after that; perhaps Tuesday?

71

TEN

Clemency was weeding in her herb-garden when a letter was brought to her; she recognised the hand of Margery Clevelys. "Let the messenger wait, and give him ale," she said, dusting the earth from her hands; it was a hot day. She opened the letter, her mind still half on the little clumps of marjoram and sweet basil and thyme. It was some time since she had ridden anywhere, and she had not seen Margery these three months.

I long to see you, the letter read, *because I have News that I never thought to impart, and I am glad to do so first to you after my lord. Your Barren old Friend hath Quickened, and there is to be a Child in the New Year. Are you not astonished? My own Pleasure you may hardly guess at. When are we to see you? It hath been very long.*

Clemency folded the letter, her eyes intent on her green plots; beyond them she saw the kind plain face of Margery and the bearded one of her lord. She must write now; and it meant giving away her own news for the first time, for she had spoken of it yet to none, only going to sleep in the turret-chamber of late instead of the little closet next to Nick and Penellyn. There must be nothing to link her name with Penellyn's now, nor

73

later. She began forming the words of the letter she must write. When it came, it was easy enough.

My dear,

Your news hath brought me great joy for you and for your lord, and I also have something of the Kind. I have conceived and our children should be born close enough to one another to be Play-fellows; is not this a gladsome thing? I have not ridden to see you for the same sweet reason you have not ridden to visit me. When it is all over, we must bring our Sucklings one to the other. I pray for a son.

She watched the messenger, refreshed with his ale, ride off with her missive. It is out now, she thought; Margery's glad tongue will spread it about the neighbourhood with her own news. Yet to have it made known in such a way was perhaps merciful. "My Lady Clevelys hath conceived," they would say, "and is it not an astonishing thing that at Ravensyard, Mistress Talmadge hath quickened also?" Better that than "Mistress Talmadge at Ravensyard hath quickened; who can be the father?"

She was avoiding Penellyn, making ready for the time when there must be no breath of talk about the father of her son; for a son it must be. She did not even inspect the books now; but at times, when she knew he was not there, would go up to the office and turn the neatly balanced pages. He was an honest steward; she had no reason to doubt him, nor to fear his tongue.

The summer days passed; Nick kept to his study, and would no longer welcome her nor lend her books. She hoped that in time, he might forget; thankfully, Penellyn was with him to lead him where he ought to go and to see that he took his place at meals. It was as though they were folk she had known once, in another life. All her care now was for the house and, a little, for her garden. Daily she would go from room to room of Ravensyard, drawing a finger across the surfaces of the furniture to see that the maids had waxed and dusted it, shaking the curtains and tapestries to see that they held no cobwebs. The narrow windows gave on to a stretch of land wooded as far as the eye could see; the sun's heat made the trees quiver in pearly mist. When she felt tired, she would seat herself at a window or lie

74

down on one of the beds; in the morning now, when Emma was dressing her, her stomacher had to be loose and her breasts were swollen and tender. She was not losing her looks; rather her state made her bloom like a flower, so happy was she. She only prayed for the child not to be a daughter; then, all would be needed to do again, but now she was complete.

One day a thing happened to disturb her; it was near the end of summer. On Sundays when they went to church, there sometimes curtseyed to her the late parson's niece, who had been allowed to stay on at the rectory with the new incumbent and his wife, who used her as housemaid and governess. She was a whey-faced, downtrodden thing, and when Clemency was told that Mistress Mary Alard waited she was surprised; generally the Rector came himself. But she went down to welcome Mary, and was surprised to find her with red eyes. At sight of Clemency the girl flung herself on her knees, weeping.

"Mistress, pray have pity on me. I dare not ask them at home."

"What would you ask?" said Clemency gently, gesturing to the servant to bring comfits and wine. "Be seated, and tell me what is wrong," she said, wondering why the girl had chosen her to whom to pour out her story; that there was a story was evident. The burst of sobbing and garbled fact and rumour meant nothing at the beginning, and she had to question Mary concerning this and that. In the end it came out.

"Is it true that Master Dick Talmadge hath married the widow Hautboys and that she is with child by him?"

We are all of us breeding, thought Clemency wryly. Aloud she said "I had not heard of it, but that does not mean that it may not be true. I see Mistress Hautboys but seldom now that her mother hath journeyed back to town. Who told you of this?"

"Oh, there is a rumour all through the village, though they say his mother knoweth not yet; and I, I gave him my maidenhead when he swore to wed me, April it was, and now he comes no more."

"That is as well. He is not one to grieve over. You are not with child?" As if there were not a woman in these parts he need not ravish or seduce, she thought; this poor soul should have been left alone. Mary sobbed again and said that no, she was not with child, but what would happen if the Rector's wife found out? "She will whip me, and may send me away lest I teach evil to her children," she wailed. Clemency went over to her and quietly placed the wine-cup by her side. "How could she do so?" she asked. "There is nothing to tell her, unless you do so yourself: and you have more to gain by keeping silence, and treating Master Dick with pride if he should come back again. He hath a bad name: do not take any more to do with him."

"But I love him, I love him so," wailed Mary. "If he were to return to me tomorrow I could not but yield; you do not know how he can cozen—"

No, I do not know that, thought Clemency drily. "If you yield again, then you are indeed in danger," she told the girl. "But if it should happen, and your mistress turns you out, you may come to me. Yet I hope you will have enough wit not to yield to him; he is not a good man, though he is handsome."

After the girl had gone, somewhat comforted, she took herself to a seat by the upstairs window and thought of the rumour of Dick's marriage. If it were true, only one thing could have prompted Marguerite to accept him: ambition. Had she heard, or suspected, that she, Clemency, was with child, she might not have agreed to the marriage, if it were true. But perhaps it was not; yet Peter Hautboys had left his wife and children badly off. What would Dame Joan say when she heard? Her fury would be remarkable. "I shall not be the one to tell her; God pity him who must."

In the end it was Dick himself who had to face his mother, and that without his lady, for Marguerite declared that in her condition she would not be present at a scene such as this must be; Dick's mother would scratch her eyes out. "She would not do so, sweet, I swear," promised Dick, who greatly needed the support of anyone at all when he faced his mother. In the end he spoke to Ralph; Ralph was subtle and could approach the formidable Dame Joan safely. Ralph gave his narrow smile.

"So that is where you have been when you were not in your bed! You are a night-hawk, brother. What will you give me if I tell our dam? It will hardly please her to hear that you have espoused a widow with no portion; what of Mistress Margaret Norreys?"

"You may marry her, and set the matter right; her silver would be welcome," said Dick a trifle ruefully; after unstinted nights in his bride's bed, he had begun, not to weary of her, but to look about him once again, as formerly.

"Margaret Norreys' father will not part with her to a second son. You have acted unwisely, Dick, but I always told you you were a great fool; now I must do your work for you, but I must at least have you by me while I tell your tale."

So they went to Dame Joan, and Dick tried to smooth her wrath at the beginning with a kiss; but it made her suspicious, and when Ralph told her roundly what had happened she was at first incredulous, then boxed Dick's ears. "You use me like a child," he complained. "Marguerite is well-born—"

"As an alley cat, which she resembles, were it not that she would forfeit esteem in the county," hissed his mother. "Where were you wed? What fool married you both? I will have this marriage undone, I swear."

"You cannot, mother; he is of age," said Ralph smoothly. "It were better to accept defeat, and write to Norreys."

"Norreys! All that fortune, and you throw it away, and here we are as poor as beggars, and you do naught, naught for remedy! Who will aid us now? That whore to be mistress of Ravensyard, and I may live to see it—"

"Do not speak so of my wife, madam." Dick drew himself up, and Ralph grinned in his sleeve. Suddenly Dame Joan threw up her hands and ceased her tantrum. "Well, the thing's done, and naught will undo it. May God forgive me that I fathered a lecher and poltroon—"

"Nay, fair mother, *I* am no poltroon," smiled Ralph, sliding her arm in his. The blue eyes glared at him.

"You! You are a man with no lusts at all; I do not know of any like you nor how I came to give you birth."

"Well, then, madam, if I am so unwelcome, let me write to Norreys for you, and save you time, temper and a messenger," said Ralph smoothly.

Dick had escaped from the room while he might, and presently they heard his horse's hooves, making away to Marguerite.

ELEVEN

At the turn of the year, Clemency went into labour. It was a day of wild rain, battering against the walls; she hoped it drowned her cries. Her body seemed no longer her own but a wrung, used thing; the birth itself cost her untold anguish. The labour had lasted nine hours, during which time she lay down or walked about the room; Emma Theale stayed nearby, ready with possets, comfort and wine. By the end it was growing dark when a son was born. Clemency heard his cry as the sweetest sound of her life. Presently, Emma brought him to her. "'Tis a lovesome boy, mistress; lusty and living." Clemency lay back on her pillows exhausted, fair hair darkened with sweat, but glad in her soul. The child lay quietly by her.

Penellyn led Nick in as soon as they were ready. She saw her husband's shambling gait and the fact that his eyes did not meet hers. Penellyn held him by the arm. "Here is the heir to Ravensyard," he said. Nick did not answer.

Presently they led him away. The fire dipped and swayed in the chimney by reason of the wind and rain. Clemency looked down at her newborn son; she would love him if Nick did not. He had dark curls not yet dry; later they would lighten to chestnut. What the colour of his eyes would be she could not yet tell; supposing they were fiery and dark, like his true father's? But later, when they opened on the world, they were a gentle brown; it might have been Nick's very colouring. She thanked God for that and because the baby throve, taking milk greedily from his wet-nurse. Clemency called him Stephen.

There were other births that season. A few weeks later Margery Clevelys was brought to bed of a thin whimpering girl with carrot-red hair; later still Dick's wife Marguerite, well used to bearing, brought forth a dark-haired daughter, to her own and Dick's displeasure; they had wanted a boy to rival, and in the end to oust, the heir to Ravensyard.

A larger cavalcade than usual traversed the abominable roads, the litter's wheels dragging and often stuck fast in the mud. By its rode a horseman handsome even in the rain; his plumes might be draggled, but his mustachios stood up bravely and he kept a cheerful countenance. It was Dad come to see his grandchild, also partly to get away from Court where the King was making a fool of himself over a new young man, a Scot named Robert Ker who had had the good fortune to break his leg in a tournament, thus bringing His Majesty lamenting to his bedside. It was prudent to have a bolt-hole meantime; so Dad escorted the ladies. Inside the litter were Elizabeth Talmadge, going to her daughter Marguerite; and opposite her red-eyed Alice, whose young husband had lately died of a chill caught in the wet weather. Alice was less lovely than Clemency; she had a weak mouth and her hair was less silver-gilt than flaxen. But she was unhappy, and accordingly did not look her best. Aunt Talmadge had dragged her on this journey, scolding her. "You have a sister who loves you; why not go to her? That is what Gregory would have had you do." But at the mention of Gregory's name Alice had burst out weeping again, and Elizabeth, exasperated, had seen to her scant baggage and had herself furnished her with money, this being short, as always. Now, Alice was like a package which has nothing to say about where it may be bestowed. She was listless on the journey, and Elizabeth had to stick her head out into the rain, to Mark Holles, if she wanted any cheerful talk. But for the most part they travelled in silence.

"I grow impatient to see the young master, as much so as my own grandchild," Elizabeth vouchsafed presently. A tear stole down Alice's cheek.

"Both mine failed, the first very early on, the next at birth. There is nothing to bring me joy now Gregory hath gone."

"Joy comes to those who seek it," said Elizabeth briskly. "You will like to dandle Clemency's boy."

"It will but remind me of what I had hoped for, and have lost."

"Well, if you will take no cheer from me, pretend to it for Clemency's sake; she will hardly have recovered from childbed, and will be in no state to give counsel."

"I will try," said poor Alice, and the litter swayed on its way. Soon Ravensyard was sighted, and as before they alighted beyond the wall and made their way on foot, skirts held high to avoid the wet, across the small outer court and into the doorway. Penellyn met them, bowing courteously.

"There is food ready, if you should need it." He took Dad's sopping cloak and hat. "My mistress says that she will be glad if you visit her after you have eaten."

"She is well?"

"Very well, and the child also."

Nobody asked about Nick; evidently he was not so well, or he would have been at the door to welcome them also. But one did not enquire too much of servants. Elizabeth nodded her thanks for the food, for they were hungry; all three set to, and Dad did full justice to a meat-bone and a pasty. Alice ate little, picking at her food. "Try to eat," said Elizabeth. "It will serve no purpose to make yourself ill."

Presently she rose and asked to travel on to Hautboys. The others followed her into the birth-chamber. Clemency was sitting up on her day-bed, looking well, the baby was by her, having just been fed by its nurse, the small Welshwoman who curtsied and left at Clemency's signal.

They kissed the mother, then bent over the child. "I believe he is like Dad," said Alice, for the first time showing interest in something beyond her woes. Mark Holles picked up his grandchild, dandling him and laughing at him, showing his own teeth which were still sound and white. Clemency lay back, signalling to Alice to sit by her at the bed's edge. "Dear, I grieve at your news," she said. "I am glad that you have come to me."

"I fear I am but a useless burden—"

"Never that; I shall be glad of your company. Here I am alone among men, in especial this last, who taketh all my leisure." She smiled proudly; it had been a relief to her that Aunt Talmadge saw nothing amiss with the child through her sharp eyes. If only Nick would come out of his library, and be as he was used! Perhaps, with gentle Alice here, they could cozen him between them.

If she had known, Aunt Talmadge had scented trouble; not giving it a name at first, but thinking about it, slowly and with tenacity, on her journey. Her position was tenuous; had it been a boy Marguerite bore, she would have had more reason to hate the scrap of humanity Mark was still dandling at Ravensyard. As it was, a girl could make small difference. But next time . . . "And who is the father?" she wondered. If it were Nick, he would have shown himself, surely; and if not, then . . .

There were many young men who would have been glad to lie with Clemency. Why should her thoughts fasten so certainly on that Welsh steward who had met them at the door? He had always been about Nick, and now had an air less of servitude than of ownership. It had not been by anything he said, but by his natural air. Well, she was an old woman; it might be otherwise. Certainly she would say nothing of it to Dick and Marguerite.

But it was Dick who said it to her, when she had fondled the dark-haired baby who lay in its cradle while Marguerite, beautiful in a lace-trimmed cap and shift, sat up in bed, more intent on herself than the child. "What pains I had!" she laughed, holding up a cheek for her mother to kiss her. "That young lady cost me more in groans than any of my boys, and Dick is cross-grained because she is not another."

Dick handed the baby his finger; her tiny hand curled round it. "There will be one next time," he boasted.

"Monster! To speak of it so soon! They do not know what we women endure; theirs is all the pleasure, ours the pain."

"Well, she will give you pleasure now," said Elizabeth tactfully. "She is like you, Marguerite."

Assuredly she would say nothing to them. But then Dick brought out his broadside. "At any rate she is no bastard, like that at Ravensyard," he said. "Everyone knows poor Nick could never father an heir."

"As to that, best keep a still tongue."

"It matters not; the county is buzzing with it. Who the father may be it will discover, in time; some say it was Sir Harry Bilbee, and I did not correct them." He grinned. "Gossip uncovers everything soon or late, and is a thing in which you both take and give pleasure, wife."

"Then you yourself have a woman's tongue," Marguerite grimaced at him. He leaned over her.

"There is one part of me that belongs to no woman. If it were the time, and your dam not here, I'd—"

"Fie on you, Dick, for a lecher! Have mercy on your poor wife, and pity our confusion."

They teased him away from the subject of the boy at Ravensyard, but when Elizabeth was alone with her daughter, Marguerite raised the subject again.

"Indeed, rumours were going to market before he was born; you have seen Nicholas and know him for what he is, and they say he will not look at the child, nor yet come where his wife is. How much trouble is everywhere! Dick's dam will neither come to him nor speak to me. She hath never liked me, and now she hateth me for marrying her son."

Elizabeth stared down at her fingers, twisting a ring John Talmadge had given her long ago. For some reason she had a moment's recollection of his unchanged face, smooth and without expression on the pillow as she had seen it, briefly, before leaving Clemency today. There was nothing to cause her to cleave to Ravensyard now; she must take the part of her daughter.

"When you bear Dick a son, it will be time to talk further," she said soothingly. "For now, the safest thing is silence. If others talk, let them; but do you say naught."

TWELVE

As the days drew on towards Martinmas, Clemency found that she was strong enough to return to household tasks; stronger than before, as though she had passed some ordeal and was able to face whatever might come in the way of work, hardship, even misfortune; after all was said, she had Ravensyard and she had her son. She plunged into activity, shaking and refolding the linen in the chests with bags of freshly dried lavender between them; toiling down to the kitchens, where Theale kneaded his dough and the maids, intent on their tasks of roasting and basting, scurried about the faster because the mistress's eye was upon them; lending a hand with the weekly brewing of house-ale, wrapped in a coarse apron. And, daily, she played with her son. He was her greatest joy, giving even Alice second place, though Clemency was glad of her sister's company.

Alice was idle; she did little in the house, sitting generally with hands folded in the solar, or sometimes in the room where the baby was with his nurse. She was alone with him on the day the parson's niece called, for the nurse had gone for her money.

They showed Mary Alard in and up to her. The girl carried a package, and began to talk too much as the uncertain will; she

85

had not met Clemency's sister before and was prepared to be in awe of her. But she found there was no need. They exclaimed together over the baby Stephen, grown fat and well on his nurse's milk, which oozed from his mouth. "I have made a little cap for him," said Mary, and opened the package to take it out. It was pretty, embroidered all over with flowers and leaves. Alice exclaimed in admiration.

"Let us put it on him before his mother returns; she is doing I know not what, for she is never idle," said Alice, and they went to Stephen's cradle and tied the cap with its ribbons under the chin. "He hath Master Talmadge's very eyes," breathed Mary. "'Tis wicked gossip to say what they do."

"What do they say?" Alice asked, and Mary bit her lip and flushed: the actual telling was difficult. "Why, that Master Nicholas is not . . . is not the father. Do not blame me, mistress; I do but repeat what I have heard often. I think Mistress Talmadge should know of it, yet I hardly dared ride over today. I am glad that you can tell her, if you will; she'll take it better from you than from me."

"'Tis all wicked lies," said Alice indignantly, but when Mary had gone she moved faster than her languid custom, and came upon Clemency where she knelt before a bed-chest, sorting the contents. "Sister, I have newly heard a thing you should know," she said, as Mary might have done; then she poured out what it was and how she had heard it, and how wicked it was, and who would believe such a thing? "But something must surely be done to stop tongues," she said. "Do you think Dame Joan spread this lie?" For Alice knew all about that lady and her ambitions, and her sons.

Clemency had not moved her hands from the chest-lid; she stared down at the contents, gowns, shifts, hose. "The best thing to do is keep silence," she said, not knowing that this was the self-same advice Aunt Talmadge had given her daughter Marguerite. She did not say more, but closed the chest carefully and stood up, walking slowly back to the child's room. Behind her, Alice babbled of the new bonnet. Clemency did not heed her.

Later that day she sent for Penellyn. She had had herself dressed in a figured satin gown and broad farthingale; her hair was combed high in the Court manner, and her ruff newly starched from the laundry. She sat by the fire, a stiff figure, hardly moving; when it came, her voice was cold.

"I have sent for you to tell you that you must find a new situation. I will give you a month's wages, and money for your journey. It would be best if you left at once." She heard the echo of her words strike against the panelled walls and high beams; she saw his figure dark against the light. It was as though another person than herself inhabited her body; could she, Clemency Talmadge, act as harshly to the man who had been an honest steward and her lover? Yet that must be buried and forgotten as if it had never been; were he to stay here someone, some day, would point out his proud bearing and his likeness to his son. He must go, and be forgotten.

Whatever Penellyn had left unsaid, Emma made up for later. She came to her mistress in her chamber, sallow cheeks red with rage; she seemed to have grown in height.

"Dismiss my brother like a churl, after all he hath done for you and for poor Master Nicholas, leading him by the hand wherever he must go? You'll not find another to ride round the farms and make the tally, and never a penny hidden aside for himself, as I can tell who have known him since he was born. And more there is than that, mistress; who came to lie with you in loving silence when you craved a son, and gave you one, at the same time keeping his place in the house, not giving himself airs or tattling of it? Only I know it all, for I was close about you; David never said a word. I tell you, you will not find his like again. If he goes, I go too; you may get yourself another woman to dress your hair and lace your stomacher."

"You may go if you will," said Clemency coldly. "Doth it mean that I am to lose Theale as well? You had best send him to me; but do not let what you have been saying go abroad in the household. I forbid it, and if you disobey me you will smart."
What was it Aunt Talmadge had said? *If she forgets her place,*

birch her. But there would be no birching of Emma, she knew; she would be glad enough to see her gone.

Theale came to her presently, his little red face seamed in perplexity. "My wife and her brother are gone, but I'd as soon stay with you, mistress; I have got used to the ways here. Emma will always have her own way."

Clemency smiled. "I shall be glad to keep you, Theale, for you are a good baker. But should not a wife and husband cleave together?" God help me, she thought, and Nick at his books as ever, and will not speak to me. But the little man shook his head.

"'Tis always her brother who hath been first with her, never myself. I knew that when we were wed. She will be best with him." He looked down at his apron. "I like it well here, mistress; I know the oven's ways, and none hinders me."

"Then that is good," said Clemency, and smiled again as he took his leave. She felt the smile grow stiff on her face; where in God's name was she to get an honest bailiff? And Penellyn . . . but she must not remember.

Nor would she call him back, and perhaps by now he would not return if she did so.

For a few weeks she tried to carry out the tasks of stewarding herself. She sent a man round the farms to bid the tenants bring her their rents to the house on a certain day; she dared not ride to collect these for fear of Dick. They came, and she counted the coins still warm from their sweaty palms, and entered the sum in the rent-book; it was a weary business, and worst of all was the tale told by those who could not pay, or would not because she was a woman. She would be grimmer than Dame Joan after a year of such sessions; already in the mirror her face seemed sharper and more haggard. Sometimes in the night a longing for Penellyn would beset her, not only for him in her bed but also by day, kindly and honestly setting the affairs of Ravensyard to rights, without troubling her in the matter. He had never done that. But she could not call him back, or rather would not; Stephen came first, and after a weary day at the books Clemency

88

would climb to his nursery and watch him learn to crawl, his sturdy body finding out its strength and balance eagerly. He could not talk yet, but when that came what joy it would give her! And the light from his gentle brown eyes was that of Nicholas as he had used to be, though she asked no man how.

Once she had gone to Nicholas after Penellyn left. He was aimlessly thumbing through his books and she knew that he was not reading them. She said to him gently "Nick, Penellyn hath had to go away," and he said nothing, but tears welled up in his eyes and rolled unchecked down his white cheeks. "But I need him," he said. "I love him."

Two days later he had a seizure. She clamped her kerchief into his mouth and held him till he was over it. After that she set one of the servants, a young man named Burbage, to be with him always. But no man was as devoted as Penellyn, who had loved Nick; the rest did not so. She began to spend more time herself with him, bringing sewing with her as he would not talk; she missed Stephen, and would have liked to have the child by her, but feared the effect it might have on Nick and his frail mind. The days began to be weary; it was time for the winter saltings to begin, and she must be present, else portions of pigs and oxen would be stolen to fill others' larders after being salted in her kitchen. There was far more to see to in Ravensyard than the growing of herbs in her garden; soon the snow would cover them again, as last year.

My very dear mistress and cousin,

We have not talked since that time I told you about the Tredesc ghost, and I know well you have not greatly wished to see any of my kin, which is why I write instead of coming to you myself to plead my cause. I have heard—what hath one not heard?—that you are looking for a Bailiff, and I bethought myself that I can write a neat hand and add up columns, and could persuade the Farmers into paying their rents. I am honest enough; but all I have at this present is a Younger Son's Portion, not large; I feel that I am wasting my lyfe. Would you consider my Presence in your house, in such an office? I would work hard, I promise you, and would render good Account of

all I had done for your eyes whenever you chose. If after a time you
are not Satisfied with me, you may send me Packing with leisure to
find a new Steward, if one can be found the better to suit your Taste.

I remain, in any case, your humble and obedient Cousin and
Servant,

> *Ralph Talmadge.*
> *This Day from Marshalhall.*

What hath one not heard? Was that his way of telling her gently
that he knew, that everyone knew, the doubts about Stephen's
legitimacy? Perhaps not; she herself was growing sour and
suspicious, seeing harm where there was none. And Dad was
still here, and would provide company for Ralph when he was
not away dicing and playing chess with Sir Bremner at Clevelys,
for the two men had struck up a friendship. All in all it might
have been worse; Ralph would be better than no one, and she
did not know where else to turn . . .

My dear Ralph,
I am sending the servant with this letter strait for you to come to
me. We may talk then.

> *Your cousin and friend,*
> *Clemency Talmadge.*
> *Writ at Ravensyard.*

Ralph came, they talked, and Clemency installed him on a
month's trial. She would hardly admit to herself that it was not
any doubts as to his ability that made her hesitate; it was the
thought of having a son of Dame Joan's in the house. But there
was nothing, after all, to prevent her requesting him to leave if
the need ever came. She settled down, at first keeping watch
over the books and examining everything in the neat sloping
hand that was different from David's; she would receive the
rents from Ralph, allotting him his portion and the servants
theirs, and locking away the balance in the large chest with
metal hasps to which only she had the key. The weeks passed
and she began to know security; it was pleasant to have a

steward again, and she would not cast her mind backward.

Another thing pleased her; Ralph had struck up a friendship with Dad. Mark Holles still lingered, varying the time between Ravensyard and Clevelys with visits to the tavern, where everyone knew and liked him; he was still reluctant to go back to Court, where, he had learned, young Ker had changed his name to Carr, English-fashion, and was as great a favourite with the King as ever. Clemency was glad of his company, but wished he would drink less; he had grown into the habit of coming home with flushed face and slurring voice, and she was ashamed for him. But now Ralph took him in hand and Dad would sometimes ride with him to the farms and other outlying places, and when they stopped at the tavern it was together, and there was less drink flowing. Often over supper they would regale Clemency and Alice with the day's stories, and the house began to know laughter again, even Nick smiling shyly at some of the sallies. He was in charge of a servant still, for Ralph showed no likelihood of taking him in addition to all his other duties, and knowing now how heavy these were Clemency had not asked it of him. One pleasing thing happened, or rather failed to happen; although he must know by now that his brother was the acting bailiff of Ravensyard, neither Dick nor his wife came to the house. Marguerite was with child again, Ralph said. "It will be one a year at this rate," he told them. He would visit his mother perhaps once a week, his brother less often. He had begun to buy himself new clothes; not ostentatious but made of good brown stuff, and it set off his looks, which would never be as spectacular as Dick's, but were not unhandsome.

The outcome of it all took Clemency by complete surprise; she had not known she was so unobservant. One night supper was late, for Dad and Ralph were she knew not where, and Alice had removed herself. Clemency waited by the great fire, warming her hands; it was some way to spring yet, and the days were still cold. Suddenly, in the faint light, she saw three figures descend the stairs and come to her, close in line; Dad in the midst, with Ralph on one side of him and Alice on the other. The three held hands. Dad's voice came, a little uncertain with wine, or was it for some other cause?

"This good steward of yours is about to become my son-in-law. This day he hath asked me for Alice's hand, and I grant it gladly." He joined them. Ralph smiled down at his betrothed, but Alice did not return the smile.

Clemency's lips parted, but no sound came. Alice did not look like a bride-to-be; she wore a bewildered look, like a lamb which has been picked up by an eagle. Clemency could not remember what she said to them, but it must have been to wish them happy; after all, what else was she to say? If Dad had given his permission—and even that would hardly be needed in Alice's widowed state—there was nothing she, Clemency, could do. And should she not rejoice that Alice had found a second husband? Maybe; but through her mind flashed the certainty she had once had that Ralph could neither love nor be loved. She felt his cool lips on her cheek, then went to kiss Alice. "Let us go to supper," she heard herself say, when they would have lingered over wine.

Afterwards, when she had Alice alone, she tried to talk to her; it was difficult, because if her sister were happy she must not close the door against it. But Alice would not commit herself. "I will no longer be a burden on you," she kept saying, as if that were the argument that had been put to her. "Who said you were a burden?" demanded Clemency. "You are welcome to live on at Ravensyard as long as I do, and Stephen in his time will never act otherwise. Think again; is it from the heart, this marriage?"

But Alice admitted the heart was only for a first love; she still mourned Gregory Savernake, and always would. "But one must live on," she said, and Clemency left it; she could not argue with the heartbroken woman, but she would try to see to it that Ralph treated her well. Another aspect had struck her; it would not now be possible to dismiss her brother-in-law from his stewardship and from the house. Ralph no doubt had thought of that.

So the wedding took place, quietly because of the bride's widowed state; Dame Joan was not present. The clergyman and his wife, and Mary, came, and afterwards there was wine-drinking and eating of subtleties, and presently the couple were bedded. The wind rose outside and it turned into a wild night, with rain beating against the stones; next morning Clemency saw Ralph ride out early to his duties about the farms. She did not go to Alice at once; a kind of shyness prevented her, as though now she was Ralph's wife her sister had become a different person.

After the wedding Dad rode back to London, and Clemency was alone.

PART TWO

ONE

They all three sat in the garden on this fine early autumn day; Sir Bremner Clevelys and his wife, and Clemency herself, while the children, Stephen and Margery, played battledore and shuttlecock on the lawn. For a moment she took leisure to enjoy the scene; it was pleasant to sit here with such friends as the Clevelys had proved themselves to be. It was, Clemency knew, largely to their staunch support that there was not, had hardly ever been, tattle about the parentage of her son. By this time, due to their friendship, she herself had become one of the close little community in the shire; this meant visits given and exchanged, wine-drinking, gossip, friends and neighbours who would call. Poor Nick drew no benefit from it; he mumbled his way through the days now, no longer resentful of her or Stephen because it was doubtful if his disordered brain remembered anything. At times he would follow her about like a child, which moved her to tears; but he was not with them today, being occupied in his library which he still enjoyed.

She bestowed a lock of her still-bright hair under its lace cap. Over the years while Stephen grew the young girl's looks she had once possessed had hardened and thinned, leaving the exquisite bone-structure of her face visible beneath the taut skin. She had not regretted the passing of her youth; she seldom permitted herself to think of Penellyn; Dad's death of a seizure four years since had brought sorrow, but to atone she had Stephen and Ravensyard. Ralph Talmadge was none so bad a steward; for some reason he had refrained from lining his pockets at her expense; but she could wish him kinder to Alice, who after all these years had never borne him a child. She seldom left her chamber and had not come down to sit with them today. Her health was poor; sometimes she would spit blood, poor Alice, and she had grown very thin. Ralph no doubt took his pleasure elsewhere, but who could blame a man for that? She admitted to herself that any sign of humanity in him was welcome.

She fixed her glance with pride on Stephen as he manfully wielded his battledore against the darting attacks of Margery Clevelys. The latter was a long-nosed placid obedient child, with hair still the colour of young carrots; her brows and lashes were too light. Stephen was chivalrous, and sometimes let her win. Clemency smiled to herself; she knew well that Margery's parents would be glad to see a match between the two children in a few years' time. She herself would welcome such a marriage into an old county family as a sign of her own and Stephen's acceptance here. But who could in any case resist the handsome boy, with his chestnut curls and slender height, and good manners? "With a bride from Clevelys, none will dare question his right to Ravensyard," she told herself again.

Margery's mother was saying something, and Clemency returned her attention to what it might be. "I can remember the Princess Elizabeth as a lovely child, riding down here from the north to Combe Abbey," the other continued. "It seemeth strange to think of her as a bride, although they say this German Palsgrave is not as good a match as she might have achieved and the Queen is displeased, for she hoped her daughter might become Queen of Spain. But that's a Papist country; such a match would not have suited people here. At any rate, my husband says we are to make a holiday of the affair in London, and so we will ride there when the Palsgrave arrives in October. Why do you not accompany us, Clemency, to see the sights? They say there will be masques and pageants, and all manner of frivolity. I long to see the Prince of Wales, who they say is grown a fine young man."

Clemency shook her head at the invitation, smiling. "You know well I never leave Ravensyard and Nick," she said. "If aught befell him while I was away, I should never forgive myself."

"Why, Ralph would have an eye to him, and his man would stay by him. You deserve a holiday, Clemency; I do not think you have left the place since you were wed, except for short visits to the like of Bilbee Hall. We grow old soon enough, and why not see what may be seen? It is not every day a princess marries."

But Clemency would not go. In truth, she had never happily left the house itself since the long-ago encounter with Dick, and when she rode out nowadays it was with an array of servants and Stephen by her. To think of Dick as a danger still was foolish; he had settled down into gross middle age and had fathered, to his anger, five daughters on Marguerite but no son. They said Marguerite was pregnant again and that Dick also kept a mistress at a tavern. Even so, Marguerite kept her beauty and emerged from each confinement unchanged; was it by witch-craft? Dick always returned to her from other women, and her children were comely and all had their mother's raven-black, lustrous hair.

"While Stephen lives they shall not enter here," Clemency told herself, then shivered. After all she had Ralph in the house; he was tactful in that he never brought his kin to Ravensyard. And why think of Stephen's life as like to end before her own? He was, thank God, healthy and strong, excelling in all sports including horsemanship, and his tutor spoke well of him. He loved his books but liked also to leave them, and with his pleasant open laughter and generous ways the cottagers and country folk adored him. He would surely breed sons to inherit Ravensyard when she herself was dust.

A shout came from him now. "They have finished their game," said the elder Margery dotingly. As much as Clemency did she adore her only child, whose coming into the world had cost her, at her age, much labour. "Come, sweetheart, and I will wipe the sweat from your face. It is over hot in the sun."

Young Margery came obediently and had her face wiped with her mother's kerchief. The sun had flushed her cheeks and brought out a suspicion of freckles. It made her almost pretty; as a rule she was milk-white like a wood anemone, like the dead; with strange water-green eyes that when they opened beneath their light lashes, arrested the beholder. But as a rule Margery's lids were demurely lowered. To be honest with herself, Clemency admitted that she did not like her, even for her parents' sake. Perhaps she was jealous at the thought of Stephen's taking a wife; yet he must marry, and she must down this feeling she had, and make herself especially affectionate to little Margery.

Stephen came over, dangling the bats, and made courteous talk with his elders in the way he had been taught. Once again, for the thousandth time, Clemency scanned his slim and erect height. There was nothing, nothing, to show that Stephen Talmadge had been fathered by a Welsh servant with princely blood in his veins, a displaced being who had lost his station.

Clemency called him to her and smoothed the chestnut curls. "Heaven, how hot you are!" she said. "Go with Margery to the dairy and they will bring you a cool drink of milk."

She watched the pair go in until they were swallowed up in the house's shadow. Stephen was taller than Margery by a head; they would make a pretty couple, when the time came.

TWO

In October the Clevelys couple departed with a great ado of baggage in which reposed my lady's fashionable gear "or at least the best I can contrive," she confided to Clemency. "I hope that I am not put to shame by the town ladies, but for an old plain creature like me it doth not signify; everybody will be looking at the bride." She kissed Clemency and once again expressed her regret that she would not come with them to London "but Margery will be safe with you; I leave the happier for it, and it is good in you to take her till we return."

They trundled off, and Clemency turned back to Ravensyard and its affairs; these were little disturbed by the quiet presence of young Margery Clevelys with her prim ways. She had been much with her parents, and had acquired their old-fashioned manners. At the beginning Clemency tried to interest her in books to while away the time till her parents should return, as the days had grown too cold for battledore; but the hunched silent figure of Nick in his library scared the child, and she begged to be allowed to sit elsewhere. After that Clemency tried to get her to ride a pony with Stephen about the copses, but the girl was afraid of horses. There seemed a great many things of which she was afraid, and among these was the presence of steward Ralph. Margery shrank when she saw him, but on being questioned could not say why she felt afraid. "My skin cometh out in goose-pricks," was all she vouchsafed. In the end Clemency left her to her fears, as there seemed no ridding of them. She herself had long grown used to the presence of Ralph in the house, and had ceased either to resent or fear him. Yet, when one thought of it, there was an odd assortment of beings filling Ravensyard; herself, Ralph, John Talmadge forever in his bed, poor Alice keeping to her chamber and Nick to his library, and Margery afraid of her shadow. Only Stephen ran about and laughed like the boy he was, and one could foresee the signs of handsome manhood in him. When he was grown, she had decided, she must part with him for a time to Court; that would set a polish on his ways and he would be equal to any nobleman. "But it need not happen yet," she thought. Stephen was still at his lessons, and learned them well. He could already speak French accurately, and wrote fair Latin.

Letters came sometimes from Lady Clevelys in London, always with love sent to Margery; the Palsgrave had landed at Gravesend and was now in the city, and folk said he and the Princess had fallen in love at first sight. *For the life of me I cannot understand why, for he is somewhat of a little fellow, pleasing enough but with great popping dark eyes and a timid Manner. The Prince of Wales is not well; they say he doth not sleep and may be met with walking in the Night.* There followed a description of the expected masques and pageants *and altogether no one remembers the Somerset affair.* That sordid business concerned the King's erstwhile favourite, Robert Carr the Scot, who had become embroiled in poisoning and infamy after his marriage with the divorced wife of the Earl of Essex. Even in the country they had had rumours of the affair. The King had created Carr and his wife Earl and Countess of Somerset, but they had not long enjoyed the title or one another's company; there had been court proceedings for murder, and they were now in the Tower. Everyone knew that had they not been noble, they would have hanged. In any case—this reached the country also—the King was intent on a new favourite, George Villiers, who amused His Majesty by crawling about the room wagging his behind like a dog. Little of this, however, was in my lady's prattling letters, which made one believe that all was set fair and gay; she was glad her lord had brought her to London. *It maketh me see how dull are our daily Lives.* She went on to describe a new play by Master William Shakespeare, who some said was growing old but who seemed ready with his pen as ever. In the play the heroine, Miranda, was the Princess Elizabeth, the old wise father Prospero for King James, and the bridegroom, Prince Ferdinand, for the Palsgrave. *The King stinks as you will remember, for they say he never Bathes nor washes his hands lest he redden his White Skin. There are many such pieces of Gossip I shall be glad to Relate to you, once we meet again.*

They were never to meet again. The Prince of Wales took a fever and died, and there was widespread grief and a long silence from Margery. One day a dark-clad rider came to the door of Ravensyard; it was Sir Bremner's lawyer. Both the squire of Clevelys and his wife were dead of a like plague, and in his last moments young Margery's father had been able to signify that he wished his daughter and heiress to remain under the guardianship of the mistress of Ravensyard. Her fortune was to be jointly administered by Nick, which meant Clemency, and the lawyer.

Clemency herself felt deep grief at the loss of plain, kindly Lady Clevelys' friendship and her husband's sound advice. She would do her utmost to bring up their daughter as though the child were her own; as though she loved her.

Already she felt lonely, forsaken by the world. After Penellyn's going the Clevelys couple had filled the gap, and now she had no one. She went upstairs to tell Alice the news of the deaths. "She is my own sister," she thought, "could we not be closer?" The reason that things were otherwise she knew well enough; whatever was told to Alice would go straight to Ralph. The poor woman was like a rabbit in the power of a snake. Alice listened now, as young Margery had done, to the news of the deaths, staring down at her fingers. In the name of God, thought Clemency, doth no one in the house think of aught except themselves? She said gently, fearing her own anger, "We should see more of one another, Alice; we were good friends in the days at Court, you and I."

Alice turned her head, her fleshless body passive. "I have no friends now," she said, and it was as if she spoke to a stranger. Clemency tried to hide her own hurt; what sort of a life must it be, married to Ralph Talmadge?

She made herself smile. "We are not so young that we can afford to neglect one another," she said. "We must talk oftener; I will visit you every day, in this chamber as you will not leave it. 'Tis maybe my fault you are solitary; I have been so busied about the house, and with Stephen, these past years, that I grow to forget aught else. Forgive me, Alice." She planted a kiss on the thin cheek.

"There is naught to forgive," said Alice expressionlessly.

Marguerite Talmadge's time again drew near and as always, Dick hoped for a son. Dame Joan now lived in seclusion, hating her daughter-in-law. They heard at Ravensyard that Dick was drunk in time for the birth, toasting his heir before he had yet arrived; but this time he was not disappointed. On a day of cold wind and rain a son was born to him; he would call him Joscelyn. Ralph brought the news to Clemency, his face a mask. "He will be disappointed, for it makes his own claim the less," she thought, but did not say it aloud. "Is the child well, and Marguerite?" she said courteously. His reply shocked her.

"That bitch will always recover from whelping, and I have a thing now that I must do. Have I your permission to ride to London?"

"To London?" His ways were mysterious, she thought; what could London, still in mourning for dead Prince Henry, have to do with this new birth? But Ralph must do as he would; he had carried out his duties faithfully all these years, with not an entry crabbed or a coin missing.

"Assuredly, Ralph. Doth Alice ride with you? It would divert

104

her, I think."

"She is in no state to travel, and my affairs press. I shall not be gone long." And he left, still with the unreadable expression that hid any feelings he might have. Clemency went to her table and wrote a letter to Marguerite; everyone seemed to hate Dick's wife, and she had done nothing to injure anyone at Ravensyard.

Ralph rode off, and returned within the week, saying nothing of his business or how it had fared.

THREE

At Michaelmas, Clemency went with Ralph and Stephen and two servants into the market-town to hire scullery maids at the annual fair; one of her own had died of an internal disorder and the other had married a farmworker, was expecting a child, and Clemency had put her to lighter tasks in the dairy. The town was crowded, for many of her acquaintance had come riding in on similar errands; from the saddle, with her little high-crowned hat atop her piled hair, Clemency bowed and smiled to passing neighbours. The servants to be hired stood on a piece of ground near the south end of the market square, nearby the booths; the place milled with people. Among them she was disconcerted to see Dick Talmadge, alone and leading his horse; it still caused her discomfort to meet him and she had contrived not to do so for many years. He struck her as greatly changed; his once handsome face sagged at eyes and jawline, he had stoutened and his gait shambled like that of a sick old man. Yet he was not forty. She tried to edge her mount away from him in the crowd, but he had seen her and came forward; she guessed from his slurred speech that he was newly come from the tavern.

"Clemency! Madam! Your servant."

He bowed, while the puffy eyes scanned her, evidently finding the sight pleasant. He was in a jocular mood. "You have heard that I am the father of a son," he told her, and smiled, with something of the old insouciance. "A rare and fighting cockerel he will be, one of my own making. Have you forgiven me for the trick I played you, all those years ago? Friendship . . . friends, my house and yours; inherit Ravensyard some day, but not before you and Nick, you and Nick . . . Damme, *there's* no man."

Clemency set her lips coldly; she had no wish to speak with him in public in such a state, and he had insulted her husband openly. His hand reached out to her bridle, and she felt Ralph and Stephen move closer as if to protect her. "So you'll not do it, eh?" Dick mumbled. "Women don't forgive as readily as we fellows; mind you, I had y'r maidenhead that day, and then y'r bastard . . . but the bastard's none of mine."

She felt herself go deathly white, and as if in a nightmare heard the words "Bastard! Bastard!" follow her, as if with his new fatherhood Dick had lost all caution. She turned to Ralph and, in a voice she could hardly believe to be her own for its calm, asked him to hire the two maids, and then follow her to the attorney's. "I have business there," she said. "Stephen, you will come with me." The boy and one servant followed, and they cantered away from the crowd. Clemency held her head high; the latest piece of salacious gossip, she knew well, would go the rounds of the market-place in minutes. Mistress Talmadge of Ravensyard lost her maidenhead to Master Dick . . . but he says her son is of another's getting. Who can it have been?" And the men would snigger over their ale and the women behind their hands, and that matter would be talked of for a day or two, till others came between; but someone would remember.

She reached the lawyer's, her mind still cold and calm. She bade Stephen and the man wait for her; she ascended the stairs alone. The elderly lawyer who had ridden to her last year with Clevelys' dying wishes bowed her in, sending his ink-stained clerk scurrying elsewhere.

"Mistress Talmadge! A fine day to you." He pulled out a bench and stoked up the fire. The office was small, dusty as law-offices always are, and filled with rolls of deeds. "And our ward, Mistress Margery? Doth she thrive? I take little time to do my duty by her because I am well aware she is in good hands."

"It is about Margery I would speak. She and my son are of an age now to be wed, and I think it would be a sensible measure lest anything happen to either of us. It was, as you are aware, her parents' wish, though they never wrote of it."

An age to marry . . . Stephen himself was not yet near the age she herself had been when she rode long ago to wed her unseen bridegroom at Ravensyard. The girl was younger still. It would be a children's wedding, necessary before the smear of slander from Dick's tongue spread to include this remote and dusty office and its inmates. Were Stephen suspected of bastardy he would not be so eligible a bridegroom for Margery Clevelys. I am using them both like pawns in a game of chess, she thought; but they like one another well enough, and know one another also.

She listened to the lawyer prose on, knowing that in the end he would come round to agreeing with her; there was nothing to surprise him in the arrangement, which they had discussed before. For Ravensyard and Clevelys to be bonded in marriage suited all parties. "I must tell Stephen of it when we are home," she thought. Today no task was too great for her; she must make sure, certain as a rock, that the inheritance did not pass to Dick's son.

When she rode home, in silence between Ralph and Stephen, she recalled a curious thing; Ralph had said nothing to Dick regarding the slander. She had not looked at him during the time Dick was mouthing his words, but she knew well the expression he must have assumed; eyes dropped, lids and mouth steady. Did he know? Had he known from the beginning? The bright day darkened, and even the sight of Ravensyard towers did not cheer her, as it usually did when she saw them again.

Later she sent for Stephen and Margery and told them "Your guardian and I have decided that you had best wed," and tried to make it gently clear to them that the relation they now had, that of brother and sister, would not change for many years. They did not gainsay her; compassion took her as she realised how little the knowledge of their wedding meant to them. It should have taken place in less haste and in seemly fashion, when the bride was old enough to be bedded. But speed was necessary before the tongues spread the evil news, perhaps even guessing at Stephen's parentage. The son of a Welsh steward . . . who had left shortly after . . . and to marry a Clevelys . . .

Stephen Talmadge and Margery Clevelys were married at Ravensyard, in the solar, on the fourth of November. The bride wore a new lace collar in the fashion that had come over from France, and a satin gown without a farthingale, of a violet colour to set off her hair. Afterwards there were subtleties to eat at supper which Theale, faithful as ever, had fashioned, as he had done for her own wedding to Nicholas. Nicholas himself kissed the little bride when asked to do so, and Margery showed none of the fear she had had of him when she had refused to go and read nearby him in the library. No doubt she was growing accustomed to life at Ravensyard. "I hope she will be happy, and later bear sons," Clemency told herself. She knew a kind of breathless triumph, as if she had won a race. Whatever anyone might say now, the couple were married in the full sight of God and man, and meantime she could do no more. Neither Dick nor his family had been bidden to the feasting, and she prayed that she might never meet with him again.

Her prayer was answered. Within three weeks of their meeting in the market-place, Dick Talmadge took to his bed. It was whispered that his disease was due to lechery, but kinder folk said he had caught a chill in the cold weather. Whichever way it might be, he worsened, and died at half past ten at night shortly before Christmas. When Clemency heard, she almost regretted that she had not forgiven him as he had asked. In any event, she

110

and all of those from Ravensyard would attend his funeral; perhaps in that way the breach between the families would be healed.

FOUR

Aunt Talmadge, an old woman now, journeyed down again for her son-in-law's funeral. She stayed with Clemency at Ravensyard, partly not to inconvenience Marguerite in her mourning, and partly because of the duty of visiting Master John. He lay flaccid in his bed still, unaware, as far as anyone knew, of his wife's presence bending over him.

"Strange that he should live on as he is, while Dick, who was young and in health, should die."

Clemency said nothing, for there was no answer. She led Elizabeth back to the solar and poured wine for them both and for Alice, who had joined them. The older woman said little, but Clemency could see that she was shocked at Alice's appearance; what had become of the bright wilful girl who had married Savernake for love?

"We all change," thought Clemency, and began to make arrangements for their journey on the morrow. Dick's coffin was at Marshalhall, and unwilling as she was to enter that house it was best to do so. There was no need, now, to fear riding out, and her absence would offend Dame Joan and Marguerite. She was curious also to see the little boy who had been named for his grandfather. Thoughts passed through her head as she gave half her attention to Aunt Talmadge's chatter about the Court.

"It is a sadder place since Queen Anne died, for all she was a foolish woman. They say it was vexation killed her because her daughter was not a Queen. And though I did not like Prince Henry greatly—he had overmuch conceit of himself and his notions—yet the little Charles speaketh even now with a stammer, and did not learn to walk till he was four. God knoweth what state the country may be in with the last reign and the next."

She talked on, while Clemency settled the matter of the journey in her mind; she and Aunt Talmadge, perhaps Alice also if she would come, could ride in the litter, and Stephen and Ralph could accompany them on horseback. There was no need for Margery to go.

The journey was made, the funeral took place, and with the removal of Dick's huge coffin from its place at Marshalhall, a sense of relief came over the company along with a feeling of unreality; could he in fact be laid in earth who had been so much alive? For he had loved living; and living had killed him. The women sat about the hearth, where a low fire burned today for the sake of the company. Among the rest was Clare, Dick and Marguerite's eldest daughter. She was even more beautiful then her mother had been, with a kind and sweet expression for the moment marred by tears; she had loved her father. Stephen stared at her hair, which was like a starling's wing, catching blue lights from the fire. How lovely she was! He liked lovely things; rare books, fine horses, swift birds and the bloom of roses in his mother's garden. Clare was like a rose, he thought; a pale rose with a sweet scent. They talked together in low voices, and he hoped he had solaced her grief a little; to her, Dick Talmadge had been a great golden generous presence and she had known none of his faults.

Dame Joan, less comely now that she had lost her teeth, sat apart with Aunt Talmadge, saying nothing. If she felt grief for Dick she did not show it, and her shabby mourning was the same she always wore. A little way off, after the men came back from the burying, Ralph watched her guardedly. He had shown no emotion at the task of helping to lift his brother's coffin and bestow it in the vault. Clemency looked up from her talk with Marguerite. "I have never seen little Joscelyn," she said. "Let him be brought down, I pray you."

The boy's mother gave orders to a servant. There was an expression on Ralph's face that Clemency did not like; she could not describe it except that it predicted unpleasantness and triumph. As usual he hid his eyes by discreetly lowering the lids when he saw that he was watched. The perfect steward, Ralph; not till now had she admitted to herself how greatly she had come to dislike him. If it were not for Alice, she could order him out of the house as she had once done to another . . . Was that why Ralph had married Alice, to be secure in Ravensyard?

Joscelyn's nurse brought him down into the hall, and set him on his feet. Clemency felt her heart invaded by an amazing tenderness; this was Dick as he ought to have been, without evil; a golden head set proudly, young uncertain steps, blue eyes that opened trustfully on the world. "He is sturdy for his years," she said to the boy's mother. Marguerite regarded her son idly. "He should live, I believe," she said; her own attention was, oddly, given to the sons she had borne to Peter Hautboys. Clemency held out her arms to the little boy and he came to her, and clambered into her lap. But he grew fretful there, and soon she handed him back to his nurse. "We must see more of one another, sweetheart," she called after him. Joscelyn turned his head and smiled at her. "He is spoiled by his sisters," said Marguerite. For the first time, age and weariness seemed to invade her features; it was possible to see her an old, worn-out woman.

Suddenly Ralph Talmadge spoke out clearly. "I would speak with you, as we are all assembled."

Clemency glanced at Alice; the other's face showed shock. Ralph stood a little way back from the party of women, with the light behind so that it hid his face. Was it her fancy, thought Clemency, that the devil was among them? Yet she should be

115

free of fear now Dick was dead.

Ralph looked at his mother and said "Your hair is silver now, but it is from you, madam, that the Talmadges of this branch get their fair colour. That proves nothing in the matter of inheritance. It is of this I would speak."

He drew out a package from his doublet and looked neither at his wife, Clemency, nor Marguerite, but at his mother. Deliberately, he opened the package, so that two objects came to light; a small square box of leather and a parchment rolled close.

Ralph opened the leather box and drew out a miniature. "You will recall that I was lately in London," he said. "The younger among you will not know the subject of this painting, which is a copy; but my mother knoweth it. In the days when she married my father many still remembered Sir John Peventye, who in the latter's last days competed even with the Earl of Leicester for the old Queen's affections. For a year or so he was supreme, till Essex came to displace him in her favour. A handsome man, is he not, reminding one greatly of Dick? It is a fair copy of the original by Hilliard; I had an artist depict it as soon as I heard of the birth of a son to my . . . half-brother."

A strangled sound came from Marguerite; Dame Joan sat as still as the dead. Elizabeth Talmadge said "Your half-brother? But you had none; Dick Talmadge was your full brother, in the sight of God."

"God knoweth many things, madam, and He knoweth also that when her husband Joscelyn Talmadge was away in the Queen's wars, my mother had Sir John often enough in her chamber and conceived a son by him. The old Queen's displeasure caused her to leave Court."

"You lie," said Dame Joan in a hoarse voice. "Do you stand there and call me, your mother, a whore?"

"Ay, madam, and with the more heart in that all my childhood, and maybe still, you cherished the son John Peventye had made on you to the exclusion of myself, who am your true heir and that of Joscelyn Talmadge. Now, I claim my inheritance."

"You lie in your throat. There is no proof of so monstrous a

116

tale." Dame Joan's eyes had grown dull and of a sudden she looked a hundred years old. Ralph laughed, and unrolled the parchment.

"You had a waiting-woman named Elizabeth Thynne in those days, is it not so? I found her in London after some searching; and caused her to swear before an attorney that she saw you and Sir John together in your chamber seven times. You were very fair in those days, madam; your roseleaf skin and golden hair might make any man forget Queen Bess, and you had been married perhaps against your will."

"For shame, to treat your mother so, and at such a time." It was Aunt Talmadge who spoke, her black eyes glittering with contempt. She made to cast an arm about Joan, who brushed it off and continued to sit stiffly upright in her chair. Marguerite had broken into sobbing. On hearing the sound, Ralph laughed. "That is as may be, but it will secure me my inheritance," he said. "I would not have cared to match my weight with Dick; he would have killed me. A prudent man waits till the right moment. I am not prepared to watch Dick's son grow to manhood before stating my claim."

He dangled the parchment between his fingers. "Well, ladies?" he said. "Will no one look at the painting or peruse the lawyer's scrip?"

"You are a devil," said Clemency, and he rounded on her. "I? When you, my mistress, lay with your Welsh steward to get yourself a son to inherit? To which bastard line must Ravensyard pass? I say it is mine, and my sons' after me."

"Will you have no mercy?" sobbed poor Alice, face bleached as a bone. Dame Joan rose and left the hall, her black weeds trailing. There was turmoil and sobbing among the women; among them all, only young Stephen and Clare Talmadge remained in their places. Clare took Stephen's hand. "Do not fret," she said gently. "It will pass in time."

When they had won home again Stephen, his cheeks flaming, came to his mother and said "Is it true that I am bastard get?" Shame veiled his brown eyes; she remembered his happy laughter and his gentle ways that were so like the father's she dared not recall.

She faced him, setting her slim hands on his shoulders. "You may hear me swear this," she said. "If anyone living hath a better claim to Ravensyard than the rest, it is yourself."

He was of the ancient blood, and it was truth she told him. She consoled herself with that.

Alice had lain still and silent on the journey home, but once in the hall again she began to tremble and shiver. Ralph was still out with the horses; Clemency had exchanged no words with him on the journey. She put her arms about Alice and guided her up to her chamber. Once there, forgetting her own weariness, she began to unlace and undress the poor woman, who suffered herself to be handled like a doll, finally being laid on her bed. Once on the pillows, tears gathered in Alice's eyes and she began to weep. Clemency knelt by her to try to comfort her.

"But for me—'tis useless to speak—but for me you could tell Ralph to be gone from here, but he knoweth that while I live you will not, for kindness, put us out. And little Joscelyn whom I saw this day—ah, I can never bear Ralph a living child! I think that but for the use I mentioned he would have rid himself of me long ere now. I think that as you say he hath a devil. To speak to you so, who have been kindness itself to us!" She flung up her thin hands over her face; the tears seeped between her fingers, soaking the sheet.

"Do not think yourself a burden," said Clemency slowly. "Ralph works for all he hath. As a steward I could not better him."

"But to say to your face—in the hearing of others—that you—that you—"

"He traduced his own mother; why should I expect to be spared? Do you suppose, Alice, that in the end rumour makes any difference?"

"But Ralph—if he should spread this evil—"

"Have no fear; if he doth not, then Marguerite will," said Clemency drily. "She must do so for her own sake and

Joscelyn's."

Despite her words to Alice she sent for Ralph to come to her.
When he came, his manner was neither servile nor proud; he
was as usual, as if the words he had spoken were again unsaid,
and he her bailiff. But the time had come to end that, she had
decided.

She told him what was in her mind, with quiet firmness. "I
would not see you and my sister homeless, but I can no longer
endure to have you about me after your words today."

"I am sorry for it." He might have been passing a remark
about the weather. Clemency opened her eyes and stared full at
him. "I believe I spoke truth when I said you had a devil," she
told him. "He may have his freedom at Clevelys from
tomorrow; you shall both go there. I shall ask Larkin—" this
was the Clevelys steward—"to come here in your place."

"I will not agree to that. I have my rightful place here, at
Ravensyard. Do you suppose it pleaseth me to call your bastard
master?"

"Then why do you stay?"

"Because the house is mine, and I care for it and tend it. It is
you and your son who live here of my charity, not I of yours."

"You should pay more heed to your tongue—ay, and today
you should have heeded it. To speak as you did to women in
distress, and to me, your mistress! Even otherwise it had been
unkind."

"You are not my mistress, although I allow you the place. I
am the heir of Ravensyard after Nicholas Talmadge who sitteth
demented abovestairs, and I claim my right."

She clenched her hands, grasping uselessly at the stuff of her
travelling-gown. "Must I have you thrown from here by force?"

"If you do, I will soon find a lawyer to reinstate me. And will
you throw your sister from here also?" He smiled. "We are one
flesh, as you know."

"Poor Alice suffers enough. In the name of God, what
manner of man are you?"

"Indeed, such a man as myself; I know of none other. What

else I know I know; one of the things I could tell you, but will not, is where Penellyn may be at this moment. Much could befall him; he is low-born, and no magistrate would trouble greatly with his fate when he hath few friends to aid him."

She felt the colour ebb and flow in her face. "Leave me now," she said in a choking voice. She knew now, as well as he, that she could not displace him from his position as steward of Ravens-yard.

FIVE

In after years Clemency saw, remembering, that Ralph's blackmail once stated remained as it was, spoken of no further; yet the situation persisted, and she never forgot the claim he had made, although she did not alter her manner to him or, after that night, he to her.

Marguerite's blackmail was more gradual. By the time Clemency understood their respective positions, it was too late to mend them.

It seemed only the following day, though it could not be so by reason of her mourning, that Marguerite rode to Ravensyard, all her raven-haired daughters about her, a pretty brood; Clare and Katherine, Isabel and Anne and Marie. Stephen sought out Clare at once, and they roamed the gardens. Yet was it not later, much later, that Stephen thought to roam in gardens with Clare? Much had happened between times; the old King died and the new Charles the First ruled England, with his great mournful eyes like his father's and his stammer that he had tried manfully to conquer, and his superb horsemanship that he had forced himself to from a delicate boy. Stephen rode to Court for the royal wedding to the pretty little French princess whose

121

name nobody in England could pronounce, so Stephen must have grown from the boy with flushed cheeks who had asked "Mother, am I of bastard get?" Somewhere between the two happenings, Stephen had become a young man; a young man brown and handsome of laughing countenance, erect and lissom as a tree; his curly hair dressed in the way the King had made fashionable, with a love-lock over one shoulder and the rest flowing loose; Stephen, in the broad plumed hats the new Queen had brought from France, replacing the old fussy fashions with graceful flowing lines and rich collars of lace. Stephen, on horseback rivalling the King; Stephen, an adept in the dance when company met, or with his long fingers strumming at a lute as, long ago, another's had strummed a Welsh harp while she, Clemency, danced. But she was too old to dance now.

Stephen. Marguerite. When in all those years had she said the thing Clemency should have known, one day, she would say, now things had been heard that should not have been? The women had all kept silence; Dame Joan, dead long since of a seizure; Marguerite herself, concerned to husband the inheritance; Aunt Talmadge, out of loyalty; poor Alice, out of fear.

Whenever it had been, it was a summer's day; the casements had been flung wide and there was the buzzing of bees to be heard from the garden. Marguerite and she had sat together in the solar and for the first time, as though the other had worn a mask, Clemency had seen ugliness and death behind the fair face, the tiny network of wrinkles about the eyes which one would not note except in full sun.

"I would not have spoken of it further, but I wanted to come to you and say how foolish I think all this anger to be, and envy over Ravensyard. Where doth it lead us, except into lawsuits? Can we not be friends, you and your son, I and mine?"

Little Joscelyn must have been there with them; Clemency could recall the sun shining on his hair. "Truth to tell," Marguerite was continuing, "Ralph wearied me rather than angered me with his talk; I was not myself, moreover, because of poor Dick so lately dead. But that is all done . . . I'd as soon forget it all." Then she made it evident that nothing would be forgotten, not a word.

She had seated herself without haste, disposing her skirts gracefully. There was still no trace of grey in the black hair; some women were so, or else it might be by means of black lead, or witchcraft. Clemency had looked out of the window to where Clare stood with Stephen, young Margery near them but taking no part in the talk. Clare was unlike her mother in that her beauty came from within; she was careless about binding up her shining hair and it was dishevelled after the ride, and her lips and cheeks were flushed with health. She wore a blue riding-gown that had seen much wear, and Stephen stood and looked as though she were attired as a queen. Margery stood smugly by; nothing would ever disturb her self-satisfaction, Clemency thought with a little spurt of irritation. Did she think that because she was wed to Stephen she could never lose him?

"How tall Stephen is!" came Marguerite's voice; could it have been on the same visit? The air had grown cold, and they sat by the fire in the hall. Marguerite's hands, short-fingered and lacking rings, were stretched out to the blaze. Where were the young people? It was all in mists in her mind, as though layers of cobwebby stuff separated one memory from the last . . . "He tops my two eldest by half a head. The Hautboys were never more than middle height. Why do you and Margery not show Clare the new bed-curtains, Stephen? Your mother hath worked at them valiantly, and I have much to say to her."

"Concerning us, madam?" Stephen was very fine that day, in a new coat of green stuff which became him. He also wore a rapier, and liked to make thrusts with it.

"Concerning you, you rogue; who else? Clemency, forgive my ordering them in your house; but with so many of them to dispose of it is hard to have a word with you. Count the stitches in each pasque-flower, Stephen, and thank God you are no woman."

So they had departed, followed by Margery with her trailing gait; and their arms were entwined before they had left the hall. After they had gone Marguerite darted a sharp glance at

Clemency. "You see, do you not?" she asked. "They love one another well. Why may they not wed?"

"Stephen is already wed to Margery."

"A childhood marriage, not consummated yet! 'Twould be readily undone."

"I must keep faith with her father and mother."

"For the money, my dear, or the name?"

Clemency flushed. "You anger me. May one not have friends?"

"In high places, certainly. Yet you have made . . . friends . . . also with the low-born, for a purpose, have you not?"

"How dare you speak so?"

"Because it is true. Why, do not fly at me; you are no better and no worse than the rest of us. You heard, as well as I, what Ralph said to disinherit both my son and yours. If we were to repair it by a marriage between your Stephen and my Clare, who are inclined to it already, it would right the balance, and the injustice. There is enough gold in Ravensyard coffers to atone for the loss of Clevelys, and we could find the wretched girl another husband; moreover, between the pair of us we could oust Ralph."

"It is not to be thought of."

"But think of it."

The young people must have returned downstairs by the tower, for they could hear voices and laughter; presently they returned, Clare radiant as if she had been kissed, Stephen flushed with pleasure, Margery tagging behind, wordless and prim. Stephen's eyes were on Clare's white neck.

Yes, he must have reached manhood by then . . .

124

SIX

"The time hath come for you to consummate your marriage. You will go with Margery to Clevelys; spend a little time with her, and less on your other pleasures." He was constantly at Marshalhall, riding to and fro.

He was white to the lips. "Mother, I was a child when I was wed to Margery, and knew no better. Now—"

"Now, you are a man. It is more than time you took your responsibilities as one. You cannot always be running after green girls."

"Clare is less of a green girl than Margery. I love Clare and would have her as my wife. No, I will not do as you say! You may have ordered my ways to date, but now I know my own mind, and will not be put aside from it."

He stood before her, so handsome that her heart was wrung; she clenched her fists over what she must say to him, what she had never thought to say again, but there was no escape as he was so stubborn . . . She would not have Dick Talmadge's flesh and blood queening here, during her lifetime and after she was dead.

"Stephen, I have a thing to tell you that I have never told

to a living soul. You think me hard in forbidding you Clare—"

"None shall forbid me. I have made up my mind. I love Clare, and I think she loves me. I can rid myself of the earlier contract if I employ a lawyer. I have no need of Margery's money; she may have it for herself, and find another husband."

"It shall not be so, I say; it *shall not*."

She slewed round to face him. "Shall I tell you what befell me when I was a young bride, newly come to Ravensyard? My husband had made me a gift of a little cream-coloured palfrey, and I liked well to ride out on her. One day, so riding, I was stopped by Dick Talmadge, Clare's father. He—"

"I know well Dick Talmadge was Clare's father. He had his faults, as all men have. Clare hath none. She is sweet and kind, and I will wed none other." He stood fingering his prized rapier, young face suffused; he had her own habit of flushing when roused. Her heart was wrung for him; she moved nearer him, but he drew away. "Do not cozen me," he said. "I owe you duty as my mother, as God knoweth, but Clare—"

"Will you listen? Dick Talmadge ravished me that day; he flung me down on the banked leaves and took me against my will. Can you let that remain in your mind, so set on yourself as you are? I cannot endure that *she* should come here, being half Dick's blood."

He had fallen silent, again grown white as linen. "Clare's father . . . and then, you bore me. Doth that mean that Clare . . . that she is my . . ."

It was not true, she knew; she need only deny it. But silence was not a lie. If she stayed silent, saying neither yea nor nay, then he might think his passion for Clare was incest, and cleave to his natural wife . . .

She said nothing more, standing with her back to the light so that he might not see the cruel anguish in her face, the way the years had dulled the brightness of her hair and made her figure no longer lissom. He seemed to have spared no time to pity her. When she turned again her eyes had narrowed and her mouth thinned to a stubborn line. "Do you know what will befall, Stephen, if aught happens ill and you leave no heir? This house,

126

and every penny of the revenue, will be in the hands of Ralph Talmadge, and for all your poor sire is the legitimate owner his wishes will go for naught. You know well that he is little else but a prisoner now."

"*My* sire? Nick Talmadge was never that, in any case."

"Do not answer me so. Mishaps have befallen others here; who is to say that poor Nick will not have his turn? Only his life keepeth Ravensyard ours; and now you refuse to do your duty in order that the line may be safe. You would see me trundle the roads in a cart, I believe, rather than give up Clare Talmadge."

"What you have told me—"

"What heed will you pay to any words of mine? I have spoilt you, Stephen, because you are my only son; the harvest is bitter, and I am reaping it now."

She flung up her hands before her face and began her difficult sobbing. He stared for moments; then his love for her, which was strong, overcame other things and he came to her, and took her in his arms.

"You have had much to endure . . . how much! Give the orders, then, as you must; let fires be lit at Clevelys, and the bed turned down. I am lost through you . . . mother, mother, could you not have told me the sooner?"

"I have done so now. You will not ride again to Marshalhall?"

Stephen had been holding her hands; now he dropped them and turned away. "Do you suppose that I would be allowed a single moment alone with Clare if her mother knoweth marriage is out of count? Another will wed her, and it will break my heart." The last words tumbled out with a hesitation that showed how young the boy still was; Clemency knew pity.

"Hearts do not break," she said, "as readily as the poets tell us. When you see your children on your knees they will give you joy."

"Were you never in love, mother?"

She bit her lip, then laughed. "If it were so, see how little it hath scarred me! Go to Clevelys with Margery, and comfort one another; remember she hath only yourself and me to whom she may turn."

"She will not turn to me," muttered Stephen, but she made pretence not to hear him, and went on to talk of the arrangements at Clevelys.

She watched him go. It had been for his good that she had kept silent, she told herself; she had uttered no lie; it had all of it been for Ravensyard. She was silent awhile and listened to the birds croaking in the roof. Later she took herself through the house, skirts dragging, traversing the long scrubbed corridors, seeing the waxed wood, the tapestries, the shining windows. Margery's son and Stephen's should inherit here. Stephen would never again ride to Marshalhall. There had been no mention made of the drugs she had taken, the purgings, the possetings, long ago to ensure that Dick's seed did not triumph . . .

And she had been right. When all was known, at the Day of Judgment, God would tell her that she had been right to keep silence, to allow Stephen to think that Clare was his half-sister. God Himself would speed the marriage of Stephen and Margery now. She, Clemency Talmadge, had committed no sin.

Stephen and Margery rode to Clevelys on a summer day under a cool sky, and the thick leaves in the coppices stirred in a light wind. They said little to one another, but this was usual; neither, in all these years, had achieved ease in each other's company, except perhaps when they were very young.

They came to Clevelys; Clemency's care over the years had ensured that the drive was cleared of weeds and the lawns shaven as they had been of old time. The house itself, with its timbered brick, faced them; the myriad casements glinted like diamonds. "Are you glad to come home?" Stephen asked his bride.

"It is very long since my home was here," Margery replied placidly. She seemed to have neither feeling nor shyness, and he dreaded the night to come. Nothing, he felt, would ever pierce her self-satisfaction, and the task before him filled him with fear and dislike. Clare's sweet face, her easy silences, lay in his mind

128

and he could not drive her out. His sister! His sister!

The great bed was hung with curtains of faded yellow satin, embroidered by Margery's great-grandmother in the days of Queen Mary Tudor. There were stitched birds and flowers on branches, but the bedspread itself was plain except for the Clevelys escutcheon. Generations of heirs had been begotten here. Stephen tried to remember it that night as he climbed into bed. Margery lay waiting ready, her hair loose. Her eyes were closed as if she did not want to look upon him.

He tried to enter her, and found that he could not summon the force; his heart was not in what he had to do, and his body knew it. Margery lay coldly and in silence, keeping her thighs closed. Presently she said "You have never had a woman, I think?" as though it were a fault in him. Stephen flushed deeply; he did not answer. Presently he turned away, defeated, and laid his head on his arm to try to sleep. A great longing beset him for Clare. He must see her tomorrow, it would be anguish not to . . . no matter what she might be to him or he to her. Was it their fault their parents had done as they had? And yet his mother would not have willed it so. That she had kept silence yesterday meant that the thing was true . . . Yet if Clare had been lying here instead of Margery, how gladly, how naturally they would have embraced one another, if nothing were known . . .

He had forgotten Margery. Withdrawn from him, she slept before he did, not having moved or spoken since he had tried to take her. Her mind was filled with a faint, prudent distaste for the state of marriage. Well, she had been prepared to do her duty, and it was no fault of hers if Stephen had failed. Perhaps they need never lie together. She would, she thought, as soon remain barren as lie with a man; she disliked children. If Dame Clemency asked how matters had sped, she would reply that they had gone well enough. But perhaps no one would ask.

Stephen rose early in the cool of the morning and had his horse saddled and rode away. He had not said where he was going, and Margery occupied herself with having her hair combed out and her day-gown chosen. Later she wandered about Clevelys, to which she had only paid brief visits since her parents' death. She was surprised to find it so comfortable a house, more so than Ravensyard. Why in the world did Dame Clemency stay on there? Perhaps, now that she was wed, she could insist that she remove here; Stephen might do as he pleased. There was a mullioned window at which she could stand and watch the road along which he might return, if she chose.

But she turned away. Later the steward came to her, old Larkin who had served her father and mother. Margery received him seated in the great carved chair in the hall, her clothes new, as befitted a bride, and her hair curled Court fashion. Word, Larkin said, had come from Dame Clemency; there was some matter on which she would speak with Master Stephen.

"He hath ridden out," said Margery. "I believe he will be back for dinner." But she had no certainty. Later she returned to the mullions and looking out saw not Stephen returning, but Ralph and the servant Burbage ride past. Burbage was generally in close attendance on poor Master Nick, and Margery wondered what had caused him to leave his side.

They rode towards Marshalhall. Margery tapped her foot, hearing the light sound it made on the floor. Even the distant sight of Ralph Talmadge filled her with discomfort. Why was she afraid of him?

The trestles were set out at last for dinner, but Stephen did not return. That night Margery slept alone, and awoke refreshed. She decided that she would walk in the garden, in her own mother's pleasance she had planted. She did not mind how long she sojourned at Clevelys, she told herself; even if Stephen sent her no word at all.

SEVEN

Stephen had spurred his horse along the road to Marshalhall, seeing neither the green hedges nor the sunshine. His mind was a cauldron of misery and rage; he regretted his marriage, regretted listening to his mother; above all, his soul cried out for Clare. She would set right the difference between truth and lies; already the thought of her sweet face and gentle ways cooled him. He could pour out his turmoil and she would not shrink from hearing, young as she was and still a maid. The thought of her maidenhead came and made him tremble. His sister! Did such things matter? He never wanted to have ado with Margery again, she was cold and alien.

He came to the house, seeing its tall carved chimneys above the trees. There was a derelict mews where in the old days, when they could afford it, hawks had been kept. Stephen left his horse there and approached the house on foot; now that he had come he felt a kind of shyness, familiar as the place was; he had been here many times, but today he came as a stranger. Perhaps—it was more than likely—he would not find Clare alone, but surrounded by her sisters and her mother. What could he say then? That he loved her forever, though he already

131

had a wife? That he and his wife could not deal together, and Clare must wait till he had annulled the marriage, and then . . . But if what his mother had left unsaid was true, that could never be. His mother would be angry, whatever happened; but he was not afraid of her, though he confessed to fear of Dame Marguerite, she was so smooth, with so much of hidden iron in her will.

But it was Marguerite he found in the hall, with one or two of the younger girls, and young Joscelyn playing pellmell up and down the length of it. Dame Marguerite gave him her hand, and as he took the puffed short-fingered flesh he felt with a shock of dislike that she was old, old as evil. Her face was beginning, only now, to sag somewhat at the neck and jaw; her hair was drawn back under a cap and she wore a mended kirtle. She smiled at him with closed lips, a habit left from her youth; her teeth had never been good, and now were few.

"Why have you not brought your bride, Stephen? Fie upon you to leave her after the wedding-night!" She knew all, he was thinking, however she had learned it; she was a witch, to cozen the secrets from men's minds.

"Where is Clare?" he said aloud; there was nothing to be gained by trying to conceal his thoughts.

She said nothing, but led him to a little lancet window, from which the neglected pleasance could be seen. On the green grass in the sunshine, between high hedges, Clare walked with a man. He was no taller than she and from up here, looking at his back, Stephen saw that he was knock-kneed. He wore a grim hat with a high crown above his plain collar. The pair were in converse of a kind; the man talked and Clare made to listen. Stephen's anger rose; who was this fellow Clare had been bidden to take out into the garden?

He had no need to ask. "That is Master Lancefolly, who hath spoken for Clare," said Marguerite gently. "He is a merchant of some wealth, which God knows we can use." She smiled to herself; the triumph, the usefulness of Master Lancefolly, with his gold! At last there could be an end to scrimping and saving; she could have a new gown for herself, and Joscelyn a tutor and perhaps, soon, a good school. Clare would see to it that the other girls got husbands. It had been a godsend for a poor widow with next to nothing, and as for Stephen, the need for him was past.

The pair in the garden had reached the end and had turned to walk back; Stephen could see Lancefolly's face, long and cold as a cod's belly. He could feel the impotent wrath rise in his throat. "Because of his gold, you would force Clare into bed with him?" he said aloud, and his voice sounded high as a woman's. He saw Marguerite's brows rise haughtily. "Have a care to your tongue," she said, still gently. She indicated the younger girls at their sewing and other ploys. "They must not hear," she said, "and it is better if you go now, and do not come again."

Stephen felt the useless wrath change to terror. "I myself would wed Clare," he said.

"You are wed already. Did last night not speed well?"

"I can rid that. I am not ill-found in the way of money. Whatever you need, only say, and I will see that it is sent you. You cannot let such a creature have Clare; I would kill him first."

Marguerite made a little sound with her tongue; by now she was coldly angry. There had been so much ado to persuade Clare that, for her own and her sisters' good, she must wed Josiah Lancefolly. It was true that he mouthed the Bible like all of his kind—she had heard they were called Puritans—but what did that matter if he could pay the bills? She would make him sign a settlement, which he would honour. As for Stephen—"What you say is out of the question," she said. "You cannot expect Clare to wait till she grows old. Leave now, as I have said; I would as soon you met neither Clare nor Master Lancefolly in your present temper."

She saw his white face stare at her. "Madam, who was my father?" The boy's fingers fumbled at his hat, twisting it round in his hands. Marguerite heard herself laugh. "Why, they say he was a servant," she told him. "Do you not remember when you were a little lad, hearing my husband say to your mother *You lay with your Welsh steward to get an heir*? Ask her; she cannot deny it."

But he had gone; gone in haste down the twisting stairs which led to the door which opened out on the pleasance. As he lifted the latch the sunlight struck and blinded him. Behind him he could hear Marguerite call down.

"Come back, Stephen! Come back!"

He had no memory of traversing the grass, no recollection of the words which came tumbling from him. On hearing them, Master Lancefolly did not act as a man should have done, and fell him to the ground; he stood coldly listening, as though they discussed the price of wine or cheese. A merchant, indeed; his very walk proclaimed it. That such a one—

Clare came forward alone, her white hands outstretched. He seized them.

"They tried to tell me you were my sister, but you are not; you are my love. Wait for me and I will have my marriage annulled. It is no marriage, and for you to wed this . . . this moneybag is a filth and wickedness. Do not listen to them all; only hear me." But she shook her head, smiling tenderly. He knew that she loved him and wanted to shout it to the heavens.

"Your mother told me to go from here," he said. "Will you come with me? We will go to London, where none will accost us, and as soon as it may be I will make you my wife."

Lancefolly spoke up then. "Thou wouldst make a harlot of my betrothed wife? Thou art of Sodom and of Babylon, full of sin that crieth to heaven. Cease thy idle talk, and go thy ways."

But Stephen only looked at Clare, and saw her dark eyes swimming with tears. "Would you that I go?" he asked. There might have been no one in the garden but the two of them.

"I?" she answered. "I—I must do as I am bid. It is the same for yourself, Stephen."

He turned then and left them blindly, stumbling as he went.

He made his horse gallop, as though a devil were at his heels; yet there was no haste to return. He wished he might never return again; he had the rest of his life to live through and he could not bear to watch the days passing, and the nights. Clare . . . If she had loved him, she would have come away with him, out of the garden. Yet she could not love Lancefolly. Lancefolly! Clare to wed that fish! Clare to have her sweet body invaded by a knock-kneed tradesman whose acrid sweat pervaded the bed, his white slab of a face avid with lust . . . Clare whom he, Stephen, had loved?

Had loved. Was it past, then? He saw that he had come to a place where the road forked, one way to Clevelys, the other to Ravensyard. It was like his life. Which way should he take? Or should he ride away from it all, lose himself in some city? That would have been the answer if Clare had come with him.

There were faces in the wood, which lay on either side; they appeared like ghosts between the trunks of the trees. He did not at first know who or what they were, and cared nothing; he would speak to none. His mother had married him too young, too soon; now . . . Should he go to his mother, tell her the marriage to Margery was cold and useless and would never get an heir? That might make her act quickly, perhaps before the merchant with his thumbed gold took possession of Clare.

But his mother might not listen.

The faces closed in on either side, pale in the green of the woods. One, he now saw with a kind of detachment, was the man Burbage, who sat by Nicholas, and on occasion rode errands for his mother and Ralph. There was another approaching from beyond; Ralph himself. Neither man was mounted. Why had the two of them awaited him here?

Burbage spoke, his lips smiling pleasantly. "Sir, we have word from your lady mother at Ravensyard; I called earlier in the day, but you were not at home." He had hastened back to Ralph then, and they had known where the boy had gone. "It is most secret," said Ralph. "Will you dismount till we tell you of it? I would wish none other to hear." His voice cozened; Stephen was suddenly taut with suspicion. Any message from his mother could have been given him in the saddle. He tried to make away, but the servant already had hold of his coat-skirts and Ralph had taken the reins. Between them they pulled him from the saddle, and clapped a hand over his mouth lest he shout. Burbage slid a rope, looped and knotted ready, over

Stephen's head from behind, and tightened it. There was no time for more than a flailing struggle from the young limbs. Ralph brought his strength to help pull the knot tight. The shivering leaves stirred in the wind. Ralph jerked his head towards the oak they had already chosen. "He is dead already," said Burbage. But they hanged the body on the oak all the same, legs dangling. "They will find him when his horse returns," said Ralph, smiling. Its home had never been at Clevelys.

Clemency had been ill at ease all day; a mood was upon her that was black, like the ravens' shining wings and dull beaks. Several times she had mounted the stairs to where Nicholas sat in his place, playing some harmless game with pegs, set in a board. There was no wrong here; she tried to tell herself that she was envious in her mind because another woman had possessed Stephen's body. Mothers of only sons were apt to be so; she must shake herself free of it. Grandchildren would come, and she would be glad; the inheritance would be secured through Margery and Stephen, and never, never would Dick Talmadge's blood enter here, to take Ravensyard.

A great raven flew down and straddled the stones of the court, then returned to the roof-nests. She watched the place where he had been, and was brought to herself by a servant asking what was to be prepared for dinner. The sky had darkened while she stood and after the man had gone below-stairs, and she was alone, she rated herself; she must live her life more reasonably; other women were solitary.

Dusk fell. She found that she could not stop thinking of Stephen and Margery at Clevelys, and thought for a while of sending a rider across with her love; but she must learn to leave them be. Yet the prick of unease renewed itself, and would not be quietened.

It was almost night when Ralph came to her, closing the door behind him. She knew at once that all was not as it should be; and yet how did she know? Time had dealt kindly with Ralph in not greying his hair, leaving it only with a silvery sheen such as filberts have; and his face was not lined. "Clemency," he said.

"It is bad news."

Then he told her; afterwards she thought she would never burn the words from her mind. The door had opened by then to admit something silent, sheeted and still, borne by four men. "They found him so," Ralph was explaining. "Maybe his marriage had not sped well." He said nothing of Burbage's ride to Clevelys in the morning, the day-long wait in the woods. "Do not look on his face, Clemency; it is not as you knew it."

But she had torn back the sheet and had seen the controted features, the protruding tongue and eyes, the place where they had cut the rope away. "From the branch of an oak," someone was saying.

From the branch of an oak. She said the words over and over again to herself, as if they were a charm to banish the horror. "I will ride forthwith to Clevelys," Ralph was saying. He spoke gently. "Lie down on your bed, Clemency. I will have Alice come to you." Then he rode off.

Other women made noise and crying over their grief. She remembered when one of the maidservants had had a child and it died at three years old, and the keening and sobbing that came from the kitchens for two days. Yet her own eyes felt dry of tears. Already she knew that it was in some manner her fault Stephen had died; but of the manner itself she could not think, except to remember that face when she had pulled away the sheet. Soon it would be corrupt in the grave. Someone was crying far off and it was Alice, not herself. She tried to comfort Alice who had been sent to comfort her.

In what lay her fault? Was it that she had forced him to marry Margery? Yet she had meant so little harm that she could only recall a pair of children playing battledore and shuttlecock, good friends, as she and Margery's parents had been friends, loving and close.

Yet Margery . . .

Ralph had said he would ride over there. She was dully glad of it. She did not want to have to face the girl today, or even tomorrow; which day was the burying? So many had died, and now Stephen was dead in the midst of his youth. It was his youth that was the pity of it, and that he was her only son.

Ralph had ridden to Clevelys at a sedate pace and had left his horse with the grooms. He let it be known quietly what had befallen, and asked that he should not be disturbed till he had done speaking with the young widow. The white-faced grooms sped to tell the rest, and Ralph went into the house and had himself shown in where Margery was. She had left the hall after dinner and had gone upstairs to her solar; he knew she had been alone all day. Coldly, he reflected that he would have to account for Burbage's coming to Clevelys this morning; it had been necessary to ascertain Stephen's whereabouts. No doubt he would think of a tale were it asked for, here or at Ravensyard.

Margery had been sitting with her hands in her lap; behind her was the mullioned window with its darkening view of the road down which Stephen would never ride again. It was almost time to light the candles. Ralph took one of her hands in his own and told her the news; the hand had quivered at first, then was still. He saw her pale eyes widen, their pupils small and pin-fine; she was pale from head to foot, he thought, the long-nosed face with its pink mouth, her pallid red hair, her plump white throat and young body. He knew she would have little feeling at the news of Stephen's death; no doubt the boy had left her virgin. To ascertain it would content him.

He began to soothe her, and still she did not draw away; her whole mind and body were stiff with shock. He started to fondle her hands and arms, her shoulders, then her breasts, kneading and caressing these. Presently he went over and secured the door. Coming back to her motionless figure, he picked her up and carried her to the bed. She gave a little cry; downstairs, they would think it was for grief.

He stilled her alarm; for a while he knelt by the bed till she grew used to his touch, the stroking, the caressing. Her mouth had fallen half open and he could see the gleam of teeth between her moist lips; it might have been a doll, a plaything that he fondled. When it was time, and he had cozened her into receptiveness, he stretched himself on the bed above her, and took her. She cried no more; his mouth stopped hers, and he lay with her, satisfied as to her maidenhead and that no man had taken it but himself. This was pleasant; young Stephen had not left seed in her to make an heir.

The bed started to shake beneath them somewhat, and he smiled, with his mouth still on hers. She had begun to emit small regular cries, not heard beyond the room.

After it was done she wept, and he comforted her; she must stay at Clevelys, not come back to Ravensyard. He would visit her again tomorrow.

At Ravensyard, the man Burbage asked to see Dame Clemency. He had been anxious lest his errand of the morning be discovered, and knew he could not rely on Master Ralph to shield him. He would say Master Nicholas had sent him over, that was it. No one would ask further, and Master Nick himself would know nothing.

The door was opened by Alice, her white face streaked with weeping for Clemency, who still lay on the bed dry-eyed and silent. Alice told the man he could not see his mistress; she was distraught. "What is it that you want of her?" she asked him.

Burbage licked his lips and said "If so please you, only to say Master Nick bade me ride to Clevelys in the morning, but when I got there 'twas to find Master Stephen gone. I said nothing to a soul, and came home."

"What matters that?" said Alice wearily. "I will tell your mistress if she should ask, but very likely she will not. A good night to you."

Burbage bowed and went.

The funeral took place. Standing by Stephen's bier, the horror hidden by the closed coffin-lid, Clemency nevertheless was aware of evil. She raised her eyes behind the black veil she wore; from where she stood by Margery's side as chief mourner, and thought she had traced the source of it; the shock sent the blood back to her heart. It was when she looked upon Ralph's face;

139

there was an expression there of smug pleasure. As she stared his features altered, as if what she had seen might have been a trick of the candlelight. It must be so; why should Ralph know pleasure at Stephen's death? He had stewarded Ravensyard all these years, and was Alice's husband. The thought of Alice strengthened Clemency; the weaker woman had needed such succour she had almost forgotten her own grief in consoling Alice. As for Ralph, he did not even stand to inherit as the law was, for nothing more had been said openly about Dame Joan and Sir John Peventye. The heir now was Joscelyn, Dick's young son, standing there by his mother with four daughters beside her, alike as peas. But Clare was not present. Clemency noted the fact idly as if it did not signify; nothing mattered now. If Clare had wept too much to come today, Margery had not; Margery had stood at the head of the coffin and played her part without emotion, even when it came to the reading for burial of the dead. She seemed a wax figure, without feeling. Perhaps, Clemency told herself, she misjudged the girl; was it not she herself who had also found it difficult to shed tears? There were those who did not readily show their emotion, yet felt the more deeply, perhaps. She must cherish Margery now that Stephen had gone, whatever trouble there had been . . .

Afterwards it grieved her when the young widow said she would return to Clevelys. "It is my home, madam," she said evenly, looking down at her hands. These were long and idle, for Margery had never greatly interested herself in the welfare of the house as Clemency did and had tried to persuade Margery likewise. Not for the first time Clemency downed an instinctive dislike. Stephen had hanged himself the day after his marriage was consummated, and the bride would return to Clevelys. So be it.

Solace was brought her, however. After the burial when she was receiving the farewell kisses of the Talmadge women, young Anne brought out a letter from her bosom and thrust it into Clemency's hand. "From Clare," she whispered. "She would not have any know she had written. I must go back now to my mother."

Clemency put the letter in her own bodice and looked at the figure of Marguerite Talmadge, shadowy in her black gear beyond the light of the dead-candles. Presently they had all gone and she opened the letter and read it.

Dearest aunt, it read, *I cannot come today for grief. Since the news came I have wept without ceasing, for I believe that it is my Fault. When you hear that I am to be married never think that I did not love Stephen or he me. We were made to be together, but God willed otherwise. I think a piece of my Harte hath died; When you pray for Stephen, pray also for me. He was distraught when he left here; this may be why he took his Lyfe. I shall bear that knowledge for the rest of mine Own.*

So that was why Stephen had died. She had judged Margery harshly, and Ralph also. It would take away her sanity to face herself and say that the blame was her own. But the thing was done, and no undoing.

She must not allow herself to grow a hard shell now Stephen was dead; the harm she had done him she would atone for in others. There were many; Margery, Ralph, Alice, young Joscelyn, poor John on his bed, and Nick who still needed her; and Clare. She would pray for Clare, and for herself.

EIGHT

Clemency solaced her grief as best she might, feeling it as time passed like the remembrance of a physical wound, a place that ached sometimes. She made herself busy with the affairs of the house, brewing, jam-making, weeding the herbs in her small garden. She visited much, exchanging the news of the day with neighbours who, she knew well, would say at sight of her before she was in hearing "Here comes that poor soul, Clemency Talmadge; she hath lost her son."

So it could not be forgotten or glossed over, and by the end she faced the necessity of bowing to the truth. Whether or not she liked it, Dick's boy was the heir; Nicholas would not get another. He himself kept to the room he seldom left nowadays, keeping his chamber-pot behind a screen; playing cards with Ralph, herself, the servant Burbage who was nearly always about him. He seemed happy enough in his own world and Stephen's death had meant nothing to him.

In the great world, events still pressed. Aunt Talmadge, a very old woman now, wrote that the King and Queen were more than ever in love with one another, after the murder of my lord Duke of Buckingham it had happened. They looked to have a child a year; the Prince of Wales was a little swarthy creature with black eyes, more like an Italian than an Englishman, but he thrived. Nearer home, there were other doings; Clare, pale as death, had been married to her merchant, but Clemency had excused herself from the wedding because of her mourning. Now, she must force herself to ride to Marshalhall. It no longer mattered what Dick Talmadge had done to her long ago; he was dead and forgotten. Marguerite occupied herself chiefly in trying to marry off her remaining daughters to rich husbands. Clemency could not help her there; but it was fitting that she, the mistress of Ravensyard, should have better acquaintance of Ravensyard's heir.

She rode over one day, and they met her at the door; she was shocked at the decay of Marguerite's beauty. Marguerite had her boy by the hand; Clemency dismounted and put her palms one on either side of Joscelyn's face, kissing him. His skin was still smooth as an apple and he had the fair good looks of his father; his hair was shoulder-length by now and gleamed in the sunshine. He could help her forget other long curled hair that lay as dust in the grave. She could love him.

They led her in and gave her wine. "May he not come and stay with me a little?" she asked presently of the boy. "I should like to have him about me, to show him the house that will be his one day, and the cottages and farms." Joscelyn's day might not be far off; Nicholas might die at any moment, or else live on into old age; nobody could tell. At any rate she, Clemency, would ride with Joscelyn Talmadge by her side about Ravensyard acres and make him known to the farming-tenants, who had scarce seen her since Ralph was steward. It would take her out of herself, make the sad time pass.

Marguerite smiled her closed smile and in her eyes lay triumph; ever since Ralph's ranting all those years ago about Dick's bastardy, which she had tried to forget, she had waited for this day. Clemency Talmadge was humbled at last; she had doted overmuch on her own boy; now let her take Joscelyn and mark how he did. "To be sure he shall come to you," she said aloud, "but what of his tutor? I had thought to engage a gentleman from nearby, but he cannot ride to Ravensyard daily." It would save expense if Clemency found a man of her own for the task. She nodded, and agreed. Marguerite stroked her own fingers, pleased at the saving. Young Joscelyn grimaced; he was not fond of lessons, but he liked the look of his beautiful kinswoman so sad in her black weeds. His mother wore them also. How much black there was! So many had died, no doubt; his father, cousin Stephen, others. And at Ravensyard there would be the great black birds, that his sister Clare had told him of; they nested among the chimneys, and if they went away it brought ill luck. He would like to find a raven's nest and take the eggs. It was a pity the tutor was coming.

They dressed him in his best suit of cinnamon-coloured stuff, with lace on the collar and cuffs that had been taken from an old dress of his mother's. That shameful secret Joscelyn would never disclose; it looked well enough, and he could fling his fair locks over it like a Court gallant. One day he would go to Court. One day—

He rode escorted through the woods, and soon Ravensyard loomed close, and the first thing he heard was the far-off croaking of ravens, deeper and stronger than the birdsong in the branches nearby. Soon he was at the outer wall, then at the hall door, and Dame Clemency herself about him, kissing and fussing over him as if he had been here before and stayed long away. How women went on! His mother and sisters were the same. His eyes sought those of Uncle Ralph, who stood a little way back in the shadows; here was an ally, a man. Uncle Ralph neither fussed over him nor kissed him. During the days that followed, Joscelyn found he was often away from Ravensyard. But when he was at home the boy sought his company whenever he might, despite the new tutor. Master Idesley was dull and informative and full of Latin tags. It was one's duty to escape him whenever it could be done.

John Talmadge still lay like a dead man among the living, and each day Clemency would take time to visit him, bringing embroidery or other work and sitting quietly by him for an hour. Often she found Alice there, seated aimlessly. Not for the first time Clemency realised that it would have been better for Alice to have a home of her own; she would have had her tasks, and have brooded less. Nowadays she seemed like a death's head, all her prettiness gone. Her eyelids were red, as though she wept much; and one day shortly after young Joscelyn's arrival at Ravensyard Clemency came upon her weeping, the tears running down her face.

"What is it, sweetheart?" Her old affection welled in her for Alice, the beloved inseparable companion of youth; they saw too little of one another now. It was perhaps her own fault for being so greatly preoccupied with the house of Ravensyard that she forgot the souls in it. She bent and kissed Alice, who bit her lip to try to restrain the sobbing.

"Ah, Clemency, if I could but speak with you! I have wanted it for long, but I—I dared not."

Clemency made herself smile. "You were not afraid of me, surely, my dear?"

"Not of you, never of you; you have been kindness itself." The tears started again, as if there were no will left to stem their flow. "Of whom, then?" asked Clemency gently, though she knew. It would be better to speak of it openly; the time had come.

"Of my husband. Of Ralph. There are days when I think he means to kill me." The words rose on a wail. Clemency put her arm about the thin body.

"Come, why should he do so?"

"Because I am barren and he wants an heir."

"There may yet be one," said Clemency, feigning lightness. "You bore children to Savernake."

"A miscarriage and a stillbirth. I think they ruined me. And Ralph now never comes to my bed. I do not know where he sleeps. He is done with me in fact, and would as soon be so in truth. I go in fear of my life, he is so subtle. I might trip on the stairs, like poor Master John; or might fall from my horse, or die of a potion."

146

"We will stay together, then you will have no fear; it will be two against one, if it should come to it. But I cannot but believe you may be mistaken; you have been alone, and in anguish, and cannot think clear." Yet there was, at this moment in her own mind, the memory of the fleeting expression she had thought she saw on Ralph's face at Stephen's funeral. Supposing Stephen had not killed himself, but had been done to death?

She put her arm again about Alice and persuaded her to come to see Master John; perhaps the sight of one worse stricken than either might distract their thoughts. He lay silent, but presently a little groan issued from him; he had become heavy in the yearsof being bedridden, and was troubled with sores although they turned him daily. The two women eased him and then, while Alice was helping him to drink, Clemency went to the window and stared out beyond the glass panes. In the distance, like a Dutch painting, she could see two mounted figures laughing together; Ralph and young Joscelyn, returning from a ride. Surely any suspicion of Ralph was wickedness? He was no more than a childless man grown fond of his nephew. She had noted before how the boy followed him, eagerly learning all he had to teach about the house and its stewarding, the farm-rent books, even the stiff portraits that hung about Ravensyard. One of them confronted her now as she turned back to the room; a Nicholas Talmadge of the time of the first Tudors, grave in velvet cap and furred gown and long beard. It had been hung where John could see it from his bed.

She spoke aloud. "Alice, come and sleep with me of nights in my chamber. You will brood less, and I'll be glad of your company." The last was not strictly true; she needed her privacy for her own grief. But was it not best to solace her sister, who lived, than mourn Stephen, who was dead?

That day Alice's gear was moved into Clemency's room, and thereafter they slept in one bed, and after a night or two Alice seemed to sleep better and be refreshed. It was Clemency who lay awake during the long hours of darkness.

The weather was unstable for Joscelyn's visit, with a few fine

147

days and the rest wet and still. One morning the heavy mist they sometimes had came, and wrapped itself thickly about the house. It was not possible to see beyond the windows, and one stayed indoors for fear of getting lost, and straying. Joscelyn chafed and kicked a leather ball about the solar; then he tired of it and went off on his own concerns. Clemency fingered her hair, knowing the grey of it was streaked with heaviness and damp; the flagstone passages gleamed with a film of water. It was a day to bring an ache to the bones, and fear; she felt old with fear, as if each year in her life counted for ten. Alice came in with a gown she had altered, so that the pointed bodice was trimmed with velvet banding; she had taken more interest in herself since she was no longer alone. They went down to the hall presently, to warm themselves at the fire. Ralph was there. He greeted them evenly; he had never remarked on his wife's removal elsewhere and seemed to accept, perhaps welcome it. The thought fleeted through Clemency's mind that he must have a woman somewhere, with whom he perhaps slept. She hoped that it was not one of the maids; that might lead to unpleasantness. Theale might tell her much, busied always at his oven as he was; but she did not care to ask. She seldom talked with Theale nowadays: a shyness came upon her at the thought of asking him if he ever heard from his wife. Better to leave that a closed book, and let well alone . . .

She was so greatly occupied with marshalling her thoughts to make them obey her that she did not remark Joscelyn's absence until about eleven o'clock.

The mist had not lessened, thickening all morning. Suddenly she became aware of a strange quality in the silence; it hung like a blanket, as though the mist itself muffled all sound. Then she knew what was missing; the ravens' croaking. "The birds are quiet," she said. Alice held her hands out to the fire and shivered; she disliked the ravens. "Where is Joscelyn?" said Clemency suddenly. She turned and looked about the hall, where the mist hung thinly like a veil; he was not sitting quietly, as he sometimes did, carving at wood with a knife. He always had to be occupied in something; she had never seen him idle for lack of a game or ploy. It was one of the traits she loved in him. How had Dick and Marguerite between them come to make so lovesome a boy? He was no doubt about the house somewhere, but she missed him.

"He will be with his tutor, will he not?" said Alice, who noticed little. Clemency shook her head. "Mr Idesley rode off two days since, to attend his sister's wedding," she said. "Jos was so glad he sang aloud! He doth not like his lessons. He would sooner be out on a horse with you, Ralph, or playing ball, or climbing in the wood." She put her hand to her throat suddenly. "Do you know where he may be, Ralph? He follows you like his shadow, when he can."

"On such a day no man hath shadows. Perhaps he is in the stables. I will ask the grooms." He glanced behind him, clearly unwilling to leave the warmth of the fire. "Pest on the child! It is a cold day."

"I will go to look for him," said Clemency suddenly. Ralph went out, and she clutched at her skirts and went to the stairs' foot, calling "Joscelyn! Jos! Come here to the fire, you will catch cold." She waited till Ralph returned, shaking his head, then made to go upstairs. "When did you see him?" she asked, head turned on neck, staring at him.

"Why, not since breakfast. I had thought him with you in the solar, till you came down."

Yet you said nothing, she thought. Aloud she said "Do you search the tower, and I will go over the rest of the house. He cannot be far." But all the time her mind was telling her otherwise; if he were not far, he would have answered her call.

She went through the house, bitter cold and damp everywhere as it was; the pervading mist choked her throat, beading her lashes and hair. She could hear herself calling "Joscelyn!" and the mist throwing it back; at last it seemed she was in an empty house full of echoes, the others' voices coming back, and the ravens silent.

In the end she went out, and down the steps; the thick mist swirled about her and its chill struck her flesh. She called the

149

boy's name in the eerie, baffling silence; it was impossible to see one's way. Presently she almost collided with the dark figure of a servant bringing in wood, and asked if he had seen the boy, but he had not. "Ask the rest," she said. By now she was convinced of Joscelyn's danger. Fool, fool to have let him out of her sight when the tutor was away!

She went on, blindly. In moments she heard a gasp, and then the servant was again in sight, pointing to something that lay nearby on the ground. He was babbling in terror. "Madam, there, there . . ."

But the mist hid what lay there, until one went close, seeing what was nearest; a boy's hand in a lace cuff, limp and still. It was not till the mist cleared that they found the rest of what had fallen with the boy; a crumpled heap of sticks and straw and smashed eggs, some still retaining their green speckled shells.

"He had always said he wanted to see the ravens' nests in the roof, but who would have thought he would go on such a day?" Ralph bent over the child's body and made to smooth back the fair hair; a movement from Clemency prevented him. She took the boy's head against her bosom and kissed him, crying; later there were stains on her dress. Joscelyn's face was unharmed and he looked as if he lay asleep; but the back of his head was cracked open like one of the eggshells, and his neck was broken. She laid him down; turned away, and stared into the horror of the mist which still lingered. He was lured on to the roof, she thought, and then thrust down. Nobody would see, nobody would hear a cry; we were all in the house and the yard was empty. And then the more ordinary things; what will his mother say? She will blame us for not having better care of him: she will blame me, and rightly.

She had begun to shiver, like Alice at her fire; somewhere between her and it, surveying the child's body, was a dark shape at which she could no longer look. For she should have realised a certain fact that now stared her in the face, gave hideous reason to what she had half dreamed and yet known, but thrust it under, as we do with dreams we will not heed, though they

150

may be warnings.

With Joscelyn's death, Ralph was the undisputed heir to Ravensyard.

NINE

The ravens had gone with the ruin of their nest; she doubted if they would ever return. She had made herself write to Marguerite of the boy's death, and sent it off by a servant. Then she went to her room and flung herself face down on the bed, weeping. Unlike the time of Stephen's death, she could weep; indeed it seemed as if her tears would never stop. She became aware of a hand gently touching her shoulder, of Alice's soft voice murmuring comfort.

"It is not your blame. Boys are foolhardy, and he had made up his mind to see the nest and was in need of diversion with the mist so thick. He would not speak of it lest we forbid him to go, Ralph says; and he is right."

Ralph. Alice must never be told the truth. Clemency made herself sit up and appear to take comfort, and even drink some of the mulled wine Alice had had fetched from the stillroom, and heated specially with spices. The thought of facing Marguerite occupied her mind. No one but a fool, knowing what she herself knew, would have brought Joscelyn to Ravensyard. The boy's death was her blame, and she must acknowledge it to her own soul. Ralph had done the deed, but she had put him in the way of it. That, and Stephen—

"Clare they say is with child by her merchant, and that will console her mother," said poor Alice. "And Marguerite hath her other daughters, and her Hautboys sons; she is not alone."

Yet I am so, thought Clemency; in very truth, I am alone.

Marguerite sent no written reply, but came herself to take the boy's body back to Marshalhall. She entered the house briskly, unlike a woman in sorrow for all her heavy black gear, nor was her face ravaged at the loss of her son. As Alice had said, she had others; Dick's boy meant the less to her. She seated herself by the hearth, drank wine and made play with a kerchief; but the real grief was Clemency's. "Marguerite," she said, "you know I am sorry for it. I feel it is my blame."

Marguerite's puffed white hand dabbed with the lace at her eyes. "We can do nothing to avert such things," she said. "There hath been little but misfortune since Hautboys died, except that now Master Lancefolly is as a son to me, as well as making Clare a good husband. He got me a bolt of Genoa velvet, only a little faulty, at a cheap price. It will make gowns for me and for the girls. He hath ever word of such things, which before I never knew of."

She talked on of her velvet and her son-in-law, and Clemency thought that she showed less grief than if she had lost a pet dog. She never coveted Ravensyard as I do, she thought, it was only the money; and was able to see for the first time how her own whole being had been ruled by desire for the house, above everything, above prudence and hatred and commonsense. Looking back over the years, she would act differently in many ways now. But to look back was useless; and forward? The future was dark. She had only Nick left, and Alice, and poor Master John.

She attended the boy's funeral, hearing and seeing in a kind of dream. It had happened so often before; man that is born of woman hath but a short time to live; ashes to ashes, dust to dust. We all come to dust in the end, she thought; but it is harder when one is young. She saw the others as one might stare at a

154

puppet-show; Marguerite in black as always, Ralph also, the picture of respectful mourning; Alice openly weeping, but her heart was easy to touch; the dead boy's sisters, awestruck by the occasion and perhaps remembering Joscelyn as he had been, not as a poor smashed body in a coffin. Master Lancefolly was there, with his pregnant wife by him; it was difficult to recognise her as Clare. There had been so many funerals; would one become a puppet by the end, going through the motions and responses, sensing nothing? Yet she could still feel.

She went back to Ravensyard, and tried to busy herself with her garden; the mice had been at the monkshood and had rifled it, leaving patches of disturbed earth. She went back to her room and asked that food be sent to her there; she could not yet endure to sit at table with Ralph. Alice came with well-meaning words, but Clemency could not hear them. One day she let herself quietly out of her chamber and climbed the small twisting flight of steps to the roof. The day was windy and clear, not like that on which Joscelyn had hurtled to his death. She stood for moments clutching the stone parapet, buffeted by the wind as it rode. There could still be seen, at the corner of the chimney-stack which loomed before her, wisps of straw blowing, remains of the disturbed nest. Silence brooded over the spread roof with its gables and towers, and down the dizzy slope to the valley not a soul moved; then she saw a horseman. It was Ralph, making his way no doubt to the farms. She felt nausea seize her, and groped for the stairway which would lead her down. An instant's resolve would have sped her on the way to the ground from such a height, to end everything; but she had not the courage. Back in her room she felt less vulnerable, safer; but the silence was oppressive, and Alice was elsewhere. Clemency combed her wind-blown hair to seemliness and decided she would ride out; it would be good for her; it was long since she had taken the air. She would have a horse saddled and go to visit Margery. Her hurt at the girl's staying at Clevelys had hidden itself beneath so many other hurts, but the result was that she had half forgotten Margery; if one's soul were a target for poisoned arrows a part of it felt numbed.

155

She took comfort in riding through the clear day. Before she left she had looked in on Nicholas, kissed him and shifted one or two of the pegs with which he played. He was like a child now, with a child's dependence on her; any resentment had long gone. Burbage was sitting with him in case he needed aught. She rode on till the great brick mass of Clevelys sprawled before her, beyond its trees. Gently she cantered up the drive; how long was it since she had been here? As long, at any rate, as it had taken Margery to come to Ravensyard again. Now that Stephen was gone she should care doubly for Margery. The girl had no father and mother, and had never made friends. Perhaps, now they were both lonely, affection could flourish between them.

The place was quiet, with none of the bustle of old days; the grass was overgrown. Finding no one to take her horse, Clemency led him herself round to the stables. To her surprise, tethered there was Ralph's roan. What business brought him to Clevelys? She did not want to encounter him, and would have remounted and ridden away; but at that moment a groom came out. He was unshaven and looked dirty. She did not question him about Ralph, nor did she care to be thought singular in departing as soon as she had come. She left the man and the horses and walked round to the house. The door was open; nobody accosted or welcomed her. She ascended the staircase to the solar, where Margery presumably was as she was not in the hall. She felt nostalgia rise; that was a room where she and Sir Bremner and Margery's mother had often sat together in the old close days of friendship, looking down on the shaven lawns and knot-garden.

The room was not large. In it was a bed. On the bed a couple lay, in surcease after lovemaking. The girl's naked calves and thighs were exposed, flung wide; the man lay upon her, in shirt and opened breeches. They had not heard Clemency, and she withdrew, with a queer coldness at the heart. Ralph's whore was Margery. She remembered wondering who it could be. She should have known, in some way. She sought the green grass again, and shortly vomited. There was nothing to do afterwards but to return to Ravensyard; despite everything that had happened there it still seemed her haven of safety. Yet this memory would go with her. She rode home.

Even that had changed. On return she was greeted by the servants, including Burbage who sat by Nicholas. He came to her with trembling hands and mouth slack in terror. "Mistress, I did but give him his drink of wine, which he took, and thereafter slept, or so it seemed . . ."

So it had seemed. Nicholas was still in his familiar chair, his cheeks a strange leaden colour. His breathing had stopped. The face was peaceful enough, with no fear nor trouble on it. Someone had taken thought to close the staring eyes.

She lay in the dark. Behind her red eyelids came a procession of lawyers, black-robed, grave-bearded, like Master Sarasin who had come earlier and had tried to tell her about money and her position now. There was the sound of a quill scribbling, scribbling in the silence. Why was the silence so heavy? Where had the ravens gone? There would be no more luck at Ravensyard.

She could remember now; evil had triumphed. Nick was dead, poor Nick who had never harmed anyone. It had been like killing a child again . . . how? Monkshood . . . it had not been mice after all who stole it from her garden. It was so long since she had read in her herbal, she had forgotten how monkshood could act, she had forgotten much . . . Of them all, all those who had first welcomed her to Ravensyard, there was none left but poor Master John.

What was the time? Which day was it? Sometimes she felt that she herself was dead, a shade watching the living. Those who still lived were all evil, saving only Alice. Marguerite with her false smile had not grieved for her son . . . Poor Alice knew no better than to obey her husband, who still rode over to Clevelys to dishonour Stephen's widow. She had seen him . . . when? From a window in the tower.

The tower. She remembered now, even in the dark. He had put her there, striding into the room she and Alice shared and bidding the women remove Clemency's gear. "The master chamber is mine now," he said. The master of Ravensyard . . . murderer, seducer . . . evil had triumphed, with the ravens gone. She missed their croaking and the sight of the straddling male bird in the courtyard, and the young in spring.

Could Nick have died of natural causes? Perhaps it had been mice in the garden after all . . . perhaps Stephen had hanged himself, the boy Jocelyn slipped and fallen from the roof. And yet Ralph had seduced Margery, she had seen it with her own eyes. But because a man was evil in one thing need not mean he was guilty of all.

She would go mad soon, lying here thinking.

She roused herself, slipped off the bed, flung a shawl about her and went downstairs. There was no light in Nicholas' study and she lit a candle with a tinder. The long yellow flame flared up and showed her his books neatly arranged in rows, the way he had liked them. She looked for the herbal. There was a place in which it told of monkshood and what it might accomplish . . .

The herbal was not there. She searched again, thinking that perhaps it was her own confusion of mind that had placed it between the great Bible and the Boethius. Yet taking her finger and searching along the titles did not find it, nor was it elsewhere in the room.

Nor was she alone now. Someone had come in, someone who had seen the light under the door when she lit the candle. Ralph missed nothing. He stood there before her, fully dressed, as if he were never to be taken at a disadvantage even at dead of night. "What is it, Clemency?" he said softly. "What do you seek here?"

"The herbal which belonged to my husband."

"It is mine now. Everything in Ravensyard is mine, and I may do with them what I will. If I took the herbal to read it, I need not answer to you." He was like a small boy boasting; the toy is mine, mine.

She clenched her fists and gripped the shawl's edge between them, and faced him. "You are a murderer," she said clearly.

158

"You took the roots from the garden and stirred the boilings in Nick's wine, or had one do it for you. Then you killed him. You killed Stephen also, and little Joscelyn, and long ago you tried to kill John. And you have dishonoured Margery because she was Stephen's wife, and you think that whatever used to be his is now yours. There is no love in you."

"You are wrong," he said. He was still smiling. Suddenly he leaned across and took the candle in its sconce, and held it high. It shone on the pale slab of his forehead where there were no lines. Other men, she thought, other women of his age have lines of worry. He hath never concerned himself with aught but getting, getting.

"You know not what love is in me, Clemency," he said. "Did not Stephen hang himself for love of Clare Lancefolly? As for the boy, God knows I am sorry for it, but he lost his footing in the mist and slipped, I doubt not. And poor Nick would never make old bones."

"And Master John, long ago, stretched a length of gut across the stairs and hurt himself. If he could speak, there would be much said."

"Your griefs have gone to your brain. Indeed none of what you speak happened as you say; but I would waste breath in speculating upon it, and so I shall not."

"So now I am no longer mistress of Ravensyard, but you are the master, and will see that I know it."

"So be it, Clemency; were you in my shoes you would act no differently. I have been your bailiff for many years, taking your orders; it will please me now to give my own."

He turned away and, leaving her with the candle, made his way out; it was as though he could see in the dark. She felt drained and powerless; everything in her was spent. Here she was in prison now, in her tower. She might choose to leave Ravensyard; but if she left it Ralph would doubtless see that she never came back.

Would he not have her life whether she went or no? Would it not be best to leave here, while she still lived? But where to go?

She regained her room again and lay down on the bed, chilled to wakefulness by the cold of the passages. She reflected on her position here. Would it be so great a loss to go, with all those whom she had loved already gone, except poor Alice, who must do as that devil bade? But where to journey? London, to old Aunt Talmadge? The old lady might welcome her, but she would not want a visitor for long; and the streets stank, and there was danger of plague. To a neighbour? Why, whoever it was would pity her for a while, then want to be rid of her. There seemed nowhere; nowhere in the world could she speak of Nick and find any to listen when she dwelt on his death; they would say it was a mercy.

No one . . . and yet there might still be one. Nick's mother was crazed, they said, kept strait in a country-house. Would not she welcome, as far as she might, her son's wife for a while? Maybe she were not so mad as they said; maybe . . . To go and find her would be a way of passing time. She would leave here with the ashes of memory, and seek somewhere new in which to grow old. That was a witty thing . . .

There would be no need to write to the lawyer for the address. Alice would get it for her from Ralph, who would know. He knew everything, and it would be useless to disguise from him the fact that she was going, and where. If she was a danger to him, he would kill her before she left.

Alice brought her the direction; yes, Ralph knew. It was a house in the north-west, within sight of the gaunt Welsh mountains. Clemency met Ralph by chance in the passage and she thought he looked at her with an intentness that proved he had something to say, but he said nothing. She did not see him alone again before she went. She took little gear.

She had stared at herself in a darkened window before going downstairs. A lined thin face looked back at her, still with great jewels for eyes; her hair, she knew, was silver-grey. An old woman, not yet forty. If she had all to do again, how could she act differently?

She let them lead her to the litter, and felt Alice's kiss on her cheek. "Sweet, you will soon be back among us." Alice knew nothing, must obey her lord. Bear him an heir, Alice, Clemency thought; otherwise you yourself will be in danger.

She could not contemplate the thought of more death. She did not look back at Ravensyard as the litter lurched downhill and on to the road that led north.

TEN

The journey was vile, the weather windy and with sudden storms of rain. The litter-curtains whirled in the draught, causing water to be blown in on her and her gear, soaking the cushions on which she lay. More than once the wheels stuck in soft mud and if there was no help for it, she must walk to the nearest inn, the hem of her gown dirtied and her ankles frozen. She would swallow a spoonful of the inn broth and then try to sleep, but as a rule could not; it seemed as if the more weary she was the longer she stayed awake. Unrefreshed, she would go back in the morning to her sodden cushions while the horses plodded on; had she been younger, she knew, she would have ridden in half the time and laughed at the weather. But those days were gone. There was nothing more left to her than to see Nick's mother, give her such news as she understood, and beg to stay awhile. And then? Return to Ravensyard, where Ralph was master? Never in this world.

The house where the madwoman was straitly kept came in sight at last. It was at the narrow end of a valley, with stunted trees showing how cold the winds blew. As they drew nearer

Clemency was conscious of terror. What was she doing here? No one knew her, or had been warned of her coming. Nick's mother had not seen him since birth, had wed again, and later run mad; she must have forgotten the world and everyone in it, including her son, long ago. In all the years of her own marriage Clemency had never had news of Kate Armstrong from anyone at Ravensyard or those who visited it. And she had never asked; yet now she came here for asylum, as though the poor soul would welcome her. Why expect that? She might have to travel back the way she had come, with no haven at the journey's end . . . Why had she not after all gone to Aunt Talmadge in London? She might be able to serve the old woman in such ways as the old needed from the young. Dad and Alice and she had been happy in London. But, again, those days were gone, and the new King and Queen were strangers to her; she had heard that their Court was strict.

But she was far from courts now, in this place which seemed like the entry to infernal regions, beyond the strange cold hills that bore no sign of man.

Well, she had come, and she must at least enter the house and find out how Nick's mother fared, and see her if she was permitted. Who guarded her so closely?

The house was tall and narrow, almost like a peel-tower, uncovered by any growing thing. She dismounted and came to the door, walking carefully because they had put pattens on her feet to avoid the mud. The door opened and light streamed out; she had not noticed the coming of twilight dark. Presently a man's figure stood in the open doorway; he was tall, and the light behind him hid his face. Yet she should have known him by his shape alone. What did Penellyn here?

She did not ask herself more or go forward, only staring up at the familiar outline of the man who had once come to her to be her lover. It was as though he were cut out of flat wood, with no substance; a known shape placed in her way. She tried to struggle forward, gasping out "Our son is dead," then collapsing in a faint at his feet. She did not feel the strength of his arms as he caught her, and carried her inside; nor, after the chill

164

inclement journey, the warmth of the firelit hall.

But she awoke to comfort and warmth; she lay in bed naked, her sodden clothing peeled from her, her hair scattered limp about the pillows with the weight of its wet. She opened her eyes and stared at the figure of a woman who was bending over to put wood on the fire; then cried out in joy. It was Emma, her own Emma Theale.

"Emma, Emma, what do you here?"

The cry sounded hollow and false; she remembered that it was none other than herself who had sent Emma and Penellyn away long ago. She could tell from the woman's face that nothing had been forgotten; the mouth was unsmiling, harder than she remembered, indrawn somewhat with the loss of teeth.

Emma turned presently, when she had done mending the fire. "Why, I do here what I did at Ravensyard; I am a servant," she said.

"You wait on my husband's mother?"

"Ay, poor soul, I do; but she needs little. She will not send me away for no fault."

"As I did; well I know it."

"If you know it, that is good; but let us rather say to one another I'd not stay when my brother went. It would maybe have fared better for you had you kept us."

"How do you know how I fared?" Clemency's brows rose slightly. It would take time to accustom herself to be spoken to in this way. Emma—

"Theale sent news to me, and I to him. He cannot read, but I'd send word how we fared by the pedlars, and they'd bring word back."

"Did you know I would come here?"

"Maybe, and again maybe not. There was no telling what you'd do. Now you are here, there's bite and sup; never fear."

Clemency closed her eyes, tears pricking at them. What could she say that would undo the wrong of those lost years? The tears overflowed and ran down her cheeks and still she did not open her eyes to look at Emma's accusing face. A fool, she'd

165

been, and now was paying for it; as for Penellyn, no doubt he felt as his sister and did not want sight of her, or speech with her, again. She was too proud to ask; but Emma went on talking as though she had done so.

"There's many women would ha' had Penellyn, and not been ashamed: but after you he would look at no one. Lonely he's kept himself, all these years; not many folk come here."

"Why did you both come?"

"A man must work to eat, that's why. We were in Wales, and word came that they needed a new keeper for her upstairs, as the old had died. Penellyn went and saw them—on the border they lived, in the north—and got the place; they'd have taken anyone. Not many folk will live here at the best of times, but it suited Penellyn, and they send money twice a year to see she's fed, and her hair shaved close to keep lice from it. She'd not have lasted as long with any other, for there's nothing she may see or know and I feed her like a child, with a spoon. You'll see her for yourself, when you're fit."

"Doth she roam about the house?" Fear took her at the thought of a visit from the crazed and shaven woman, perhaps when she was alone in bed here. Emma shook her head.

"She hath not walked these twenty years. It is like poor Master John at Ravensyard, except that he still had his wits inside his head, but hers are gone. You'd think she slept."

"You and Penellyn guard her well. I should thank you for that, who was her son's wife. You heard what befell Master Nick?"

"Ay. We hear most things in time."

"Penellyn . . . doth he ever leave here?"

"Maybe to ride to a fair, or on business for *her*. There's not much; she was married again to a man of her own clan, and he's long dead. The strong die and the weak live on. As long as the Armstrongs aren't burdened with her, 'tis all one to them how she fares or who looks to her."

"Poor soul." Then she struggled up in the bed. "Emma, I would talk with Penellyn."

He had come into the room and stood with eyes downcast, though Emma had flung a covering about her. He will see a grey-haired woman, she thought, and maybe in any case he loves me no longer. Yet . . . "Penellyn," she said softly, as if calling to a frightened child. "Penellyn."

"What would you with me?" His voice sounded harsh; had it not been for Emma's tale of his rejection of other women, she would have lost heart. Now, she must cozen him, and show patience.

"I would tell you of our son, and how he died."

"I knew him not while he lived."

"He was comely and gentle. He had your nature; he knew how to love."

"Maybe he took something from his mother."

She turned and smiled at him through her tears. "They took him in the end, and hanged him on a tree. They tried to make me believe he had killed himself. I felt that day as if my heart had died. Now . . ."

"You found out that they hanged him. Did you fetch the law?" The voice was harsh again.

"How could I? I had no proof, and they said he had been in despair over his marriage and his love for another. I only know in my heart that it was not so, and that others killed him. And they seduced his bride, and married the girl he had loved to a merchant for his gold."

"A merchant is somewhat better than a servant."

"You are bitter." She began to sob. "Can you not forgive me, even now? I should not have sent you away, I know it; and now you hate me for a certainty, and Ravensyard is owned by others, and I have no home and no lover."

"Hate you?" he said, as if considering the words. "That I do not and never did. But I too was . . . bitter."

He had come over. Suddenly her small hand reached out and stroked the front of his doublet. "It is good to touch you again," she said. The hand began caressing the spun cloth, feeling the warmth of his body beneath.

"Clemency . . . Clemency!"

The voice had grown rough. Swiftly he fell to his knees by the bed and hid his face where her knees were. "The nights I have longed for you, and thought never to hold you or see you again . . ."

"Now you see me, and you may hold me; but only if it is your wish. I would not have any man cleave to me from pity."

"I pity what hath been. Now we are free again. I have never forgotten what was between us, and I knew no other woman could give it me, only yourself, yourself . . . and you have come here, like a miracle, when I thought all was ended."

"It is not ended," she said, "it is beginning. Do not think that I forgot either . . . but I made myself thrust the memory down in my mind for Stephen's sake. Ah, Penellyn, if you could have seen your Stephen! And now I come to you, grey-haired with sorrow."

He set his mouth in the hair. "It is silver, not grey. We will grow old together. Will you be content here?" His hands gently encircled her body, caressing the flesh beneath the shawl. Presently he kissed her. She felt the years fall from her, making her young again.

"You must be my wife and not my leman," he said. "Then I will not lose you any more."

They were married in the small parish church five miles distant; it was plain inside and out, built of sharp flints. It was a strange and delicious feeling to have her hand rest lightly on Penellyn's arm and say to herself "This is my husband, whom I have sworn to love and honour." And keep her vow she would, she told herself. Afterwards she turned to Emma, who had accompanied them, silent and non-committal. After all these years when she hath left her husband for her brother, Clemency thought, she may well be jealous of me. She reached up to kiss tall Emma.

"I would you will love me as your good-sister, as I love you."

Emma flushed and then wept. "Glad I am that the two of you are together again, for he was never a happy man lacking you, my mistress."

"I am no longer your mistress. As I said, I am your good-sister. Call me Clemency, as I call you Emma."

Penellyn looked on with proud eyes; there was much sweetness in his wife.

They had taken her up before then to visit Nick's mother. She lay on a bed, inert except that each time she breathed it made a puffing sound between her dry lips, and her eyes were closed. She had once been beautiful. What world of her own did she live in, or had she forgotten all the world and all of life? Clemency turned away, weeping, into the strong arms of Penellyn.

"What can anyone do for her? Would . . . Nick . . . have been so had he lived longer?"

"Who can tell?" He stroked the silver hair. "There is nothing to be done for her but keep her clean, and pray."

She stared at him in wonderment; in addition to loyalty and strength of body he had a deep religious faith, which she had not known of. It did not show itself in church attendance or assiduity among the prayer-meetings of Puritan folk, but it was sincere. She knew that she had much to learn of him. He led her out of the sad room and downstairs into the firelight.

But she did not forget. Nick's mother, tended here in a forgotten valley! It would not matter to that poor soul where she lay. In time, could they not all travel south again, to Clevelys perhaps, if Margery would have them? It was the more possible now Penellyn was by her with his record of trustworthy stewardship. Between them they could again make Clevelys something of what it had been in the days of Margery's parents, with a fair garden and a welcoming house. They could guard them both, the madwoman and the threatened girl. But perhaps it was all a dream.

Meantime, Penellyn was her lover again. She had forgotten what it was to know ecstasy. Now, in his arms, she could forget both past and future; her cry sounded nightly through the close-drawn curtains of their shared bed, but she felt no shame. Let the world know, if it would, of her paradise . . . he was now so much a part of her body that she did not feel whole unless he

169

entered it. That he responded to her she could not doubt; his whole body shook with passion when he took her, and afterwards he lay in her arms like a child.

Yet when they had done, and he slept, she fretted. She did not like the house in the valley, where nothing grew. She had begun to wonder more and more how they fared at home, both Alice and Margery; no word had come.

She must have had a premonition that all was not well, because some weeks after her marriage with Penellyn word did come of Alice. Clemency was alone when a rider arrived with a letter; it had been written by Ralph.

. . . your sister is dead, and Master John also, of a putrid fever. There was nothing to be done for them. For the reason I mention we have cered them at once, not waiting for you to come to the burying. I trust you are well, and Penellyn.

She cried out, and Emma came; Emma who now, since the words in church, was her old devoted, loyal self, and put her arms about her sister-in-law. "My little one, what is it? What harm hath come?" She stared at the paper, for she could not read.

"My sister Alice, and Master John, are dead." The word had a leaden sound. Emma flung her hands to her cheeks.

"Ah, that devil hath got rid of them without losing time! Here is Penellyn."

Penellyn's arm was about her, his brows drawn close as he read the news; Alice, poor Alice, whom she had abandoned . . . Yet at the time she could have endured no more; and had she stayed, could she in any case have protected Alice, any more than she had prevented the poison being poured into poor Nick's wine? Maybe not . . . Ralph had had his way in everything. There was only one left who might need her aid still: Margery. She must think of Margery now.

Spring had come, and the trees in the valley budded to a harsh and difficult green; further off, the alien shapes of the hills grew clear. She felt overshadowed by them. Now it was light enough in early morning for her to see Penellyn as he still lay asleep, wondering how she could have lived as long without the sight of him. His strong dark hair had locks of white at the temples, and the stubble of his chin was grey below the relaxed mouth. What contentment was in her own life she knew, and yet she could not forbear to think of that beleaguered girl in the south. If Ralph wedded Margery, would she be happy? Or would the evil claim her also? Was she herself a fool to ascribe so much to evil? Poor Alice's death had come so pat, yet perhaps for that very reason it had been natural. Surely no poisoner would dare act to swiftly twice . . . yet killers grew reckless with success and perhaps one day Ralph would fail. "And I shall not be there to see," she thought. She tried to down her thoughts, her memories, and live for the present; as Penellyn wakened she planted her lips softly against his own. The fiery dark eyes opened and glowed, and they lay in close embrace; there was none to hasten them. Yet she must remember that she was a steward's wife now, no longer the mistress of Ravensyard. She must not lead Penellyn into idle ways that would anger his masters . . . then she smiled. Nobody in the world could make Penellyn idle.

But the thought of Margery at Clevelys would not be banished. Was all well with her? Would she be glad if, by some means, Clemency could come to her again? If they were nearer home it would be so different, she could ride to be with Margery, aid her if she needed aid and would accept it. One could not trust Ralph to do what was best.

The remembrance of Clevelys, and the good of being nearer, stayed in her mind. Should she broach the matter to Penellyn, or write first to Margery to see if they would be welcome? For she would gladly take him with her to steward Clevelys, if Margery would but agree, and Ralph would do no harm to them when Ravensyard was safely his and he was free to make his heir. "None cares, not even the Armstrongs, whether or not we stay in this desolate place till we die; poor Mistress Kate could be moved south by litter, and do as well there." Yet she herself, Clemency Penellyn, must take care not to seem to dispose her husband's life; she had always disliked managing women.

"Penellyn is no slave, but full man," she thought, and smiled inwardly.

She herself should perhaps write to Margery without saying anything yet. It would do no harm, and might help her and themselves; and perhaps, if they wished it, Emma and Theale could by the end be together again as man and wife. The more she thought of the scheme the more she wished it well. But if Penellyn preferred to stay on here, she would not leave him.

Margery's reply, in her small even handwriting, came within the week. They might come if they would, and bring Nick's mother; Larkin the steward was very old, and would be glad of Penellyn's help. Then, a few lines down, the girl added, as if in afterthought, *Ralph is to be married tomorrow.*

The blood fled from Clemency's face, leaving it white. What had befallen that Ralph so mistreated Margery? She had thought that even he, untrustworthy and evil as he was, having used the young woman so shamelessly would marry her; it had even entered her mind that Alice had died for some such reason, without Margery's connivance. Now, all was changed, and the uglier for it.

Penellyn came in. "What is it, my heart?" he said gently. "You have had more bad news." She handed him the letter without speaking. If he were angry with her for writing about Clevelys, it could not be helped. He stood reading, his dark face thoughtful. "You told me nothing of this," he said; it was difficult to tell whether or not his voice held reproach.

She went close to him, laying her hand on his coat. "Maybe I did wrong," she said. "But I did not want to tell you of it until I knew if she would be willing that we go there, all of us. Oh, poor Margery, poor child! Ralph was her lover while Alice still lived; he took her after Stephen died, and often since, and now he will not marry her. I should like to comfort her if I can; but I would not leave you."

He raised a finger and stroked her cheek. "You are not happy in this house, Clemency. I have noted it, and said nothing. I do not think you can ever be happy out of sight of Ravensyard."

"I am happy where you are. You must know it."

Penellyn smiled, with tenderness in his face. "We love one another, that is true, and I thank God. But always you hunger for the south, like the flowers and plants that will not grow here. If you would like to go to Margery without delay, I will write to my masters and see if they will permit me to take Mistress Armstrong away from this place. If they will not, I must wait here till another steward is found. Otherwise I should be with you soon."

"Every day will be long without you, and the nights more so."

"We have tonight." He kissed her.

"Do not end by falling between two stools and being without a place, because then we should have to be like the Egyptians and take to the roads, and I should be happy enough with you." She laughed; now that her anxiety over his feelings on the matter had been resolved, joy filled her at the thought of seeing Ravensyard again. Why was she so attached to that place, which had brought her nothing but ill except for Penellyn?

She set out next day, not taking time to write to Margery in reply. Poor child, alone with servants and her own grief; the sooner she had company the better. "That she loved Ralph was certain, or she would not have given herself to him," Clemency told herself, at the same time shuddering in memory of the pairing she had herself seen. But Ralph would have done well enough had he wedded the heiress of Clevelys, adding it to his own domain. Something must have turned his thoughts elsewhere; well, she would see how the land lay. Already, though they had only parted that morning, she yearned for Penellyn and knew that the time spent apart from him would seem long.

She came at last to Clevelys, puasing for moments at the forked place in the road to look across at Ravensyard where it lay. Then she turned away to the other great house which had held friendship and welcome long before Margery's birth. She must be a mother to Margery now.

173

Margery was not in the hall; this time, a servant preceded Clemency to the solar. Margery stood there gazing out of the window, her little dog at her feet. She must have seen me come, thought Clemency, and made herself say aloud "How is it with you, my dear?"

Margery turned then, and Clemency was disturbed by her haggard look; she had grown thinner and her cheeks were roughed. She smiled, and suffered herself to be kissed on the forehead; but all her self-sufficiency had gone, and it was as if two strangers confronted one another.

The servant had left. "Will you take wine?" said Margery. "Dinner will be ready soon." She moved to where the flagon stood, and poured for herself and Clemency. The red wine was warming after the journey. "How good it is to be back again!" said Clemency truthfully. The other looked at her, almost in a sly fashion. "Yes, you are glad to be back," she scid. "When doth your husband follow?"

"Whenever he is assured that he may be of use to you. We would not displace old Larkin. As for poor Mistress Armstrong, she troubles no one; I will be responsible for the care of her."

"You may have to; many of the servants have left," said Margery tonelessly. "There is much Puritanical feeling about among the common folk; Ralph's coming here did not suit them." She had brought out the matter deliberately and her gaze stayed full on Clemency's face. "It is a pity, is it not?" she said. "Now he will never order matters here."

"You are better to order them for yourself. Whom did Ralph marry?" It was best to speak drily, openly. Margery had bent down, caressing her little dog; it followed wherever she led, hiding itself in the folds of her gown. She is no longer comely, thought Clemency with pity; Ralph has wrung the youth from her.

"His wife is of merchant stock, I believe, but a fertile one; she had twelve brothers and sisters. He wants an heir more than any thing; last time he came, he left me a letter. I will show it to you; it is the first time I had heard, or dreamed of, his marriage."

She went to the table, and brought back a folded paper,

174

handing it to Clemency. Their fingers brushed for instants; Margery's were ice-cold, as though it were she and not the other who had made a long journey.

Clemency opened the sheet. *Sweetheart*, it read, *this is to say farewell; I am to be married in two days. Truth to tell I love your sweet body so much that had I got you pregnant I would have made you my wife and mistress of Ravensyard; but I must have an heir, else all hath gone for naught. Forgive me if you can, and remember we loved well. Your R.*

"He was at pains not to sign his name," said Clemency. "Sweet, you are well rid of him." She forbore to burden Margery with any of the crimes of Ralph, fresh in her mind as they still were; she went to put an arm about the girl's shoulders, but Margery shook her off. Beneath the rouge had come a faint flush of triumph.

"I held my peace," she said, "and did not say what I already knew—I was almost certain last time he came, but I waited. I fancied I loved him; now I abhor him. But what I did not tell him will make him regret me." She showed her small teeth in a smile. "I am pregnant with Ralph's child, who might have been heir of Ravensyard. As matters stand, he must satisfy himself with Clevelys."

She suddenly flung her hands up before her mouth to stifle sobbing. "You will not leave me, Madam Clemency? It will be talked of, I don't doubt. The Puritans would have me on a shame-stool. God forbid they ever rule the land."

"I will never leave you till the birth, and after," Clemency promised. She went and kissed Margery on the cheek; the tumult in her own heart was suddenly at peace. It had not been in vain to dream of bringing Penellyn and Emma south. Margery would be glad of them.

ELEVEN

Clemency agreed with Margery that it was best to go on as if nothing were amiss, and that same Sunday they attended church together. Ralph was there, with his wife in a plume-laden hat; the outline of her cheek beneath it was plump and had a high colour. At the lych-gate afterwards, many assembled to meet the bride; but the two women from Clevelys kept to themselves, confining their gossip to old friends who came to wish Clemency well now that she was back again. Her marriage was no longer news by now, and anyone who resented her fall from lady of Ravensyard to wife of a steward might do so, she thought; but nothing showed of this. It was pleasant to meet old friends again; eccentric Lady Hawkyard, who still dressed as they had done in the days of Queen Bess, with a high ruff and grimy jewels in her hair; old Sir Harry Bilbee, who was vociferous about this new tax the King was demanding to help him build ships. "The King's the King, and those who murmur 'ud be better staying silent," he informed the company, adding that some damned squire named Hampden had refused to pay the ship-money tax, and folk said would land himself in gaol. "What are things coming to, that men question the way the

King reigneth? The old Queen's father would ha' had their heads as well as their money." And he bumbled on about the extravagance of the late King James, which his son nowhere matched except for buying paintings from foreign parts. The lych-gate had become crowded by then with knots of broad hats, and Clemency and Margery excused themselves; they walked together in silence on the way home, except for the talk that stemmed from one remark of Margery's.

"I did not wish to meet his bride; was it wrong, think you? I would put a brave face on it, but I do not care to look on Ralph and he, no doubt, is the same."

"You acted rightly; there should be no visiting now between Clevelys and Ravensyard, and Ralph's wife may be too greatly eager to make such acquaintance as she can."

"If he hath got himself a termagant, it serves him right. I wonder if the heir is made yet?"

"Not so soon, surely."

"Many a babe hath been born of wedding nights. Ralph shall see my heir coming ere his own. I hope he will sit in church and see it. It would be fit punishment for him if his wife proves barren."

"Do not think of punishments, but only of your health," Clemency begged. She looked at Margery sadly; this bitter, defiant woman was much changed from the smug little person who had been married to Stephen long ago. As though she had read Clemency's thoughts, the other spoke of him.

"If my child be a son, as I hope, I shall call him after Stephen. Would that please you?"

"It would please me greatly."

"Poor Stephen," said Margery suddenly, "I should beg your pardon for the way I treated him. The truth was that he loved me not. Nor did Ralph, it seems. Alack that I am so little loveable! It is too late now to change, for I have spun my shroud."

Clemency grasped her hand in her own and begged her to be silent. "Keep a good heart and all will be well," she said, "and you will have your child to cheer you." But within herself she

178

knew what Margery suffered; and gossip would start when her body thickened. The father of the child might be known, or might not; one was as bad as the other.

I know that from my describing of her state, you will see I cannot leave her, Clemency had written to Penellyn. She hoped the news would not make him unwilling to come to Clevelys; though he was no Puritan he had strict notions, part of his Welsh heritage. Besides, a wife's place was with her husband; and yet had he not kept his own sister Emma with him for years, while Theale stayed on at Ravensyard alone? At any rate she awaited his reply with impatience, and none came.

The days passed. Margery and she would play chess sometimes in the evenings; it helped to divert the time. Sometimes between moves Clemency would wonder if Penellyn had had word of whether or not he might bring the madwoman south; perhaps he had had to ride to the Border. By day she would stand at the solar window, and watch the wooded road; summer had come, and soon the trees would be changing colours for autumn, and growing thin of leaves.

But it was still a summer's day when she sighted the litter on the road, and the figure of a horseman escorting it. It was Penellyn! He rode a horse as part of his body; she would know him afar off. She ran down to the hall in her delight, then out to the lawn, then went back; she must not go to him on the road dusty and dishevelled, as though they were young. But her kiss when she felt his arms about her was that of love and youth. "Glad I am that you have come," she whispered, searching his face, astonished that it should be the same as when she had left him; how long it had seemed!

"And I am glad to be here, with you. Emma is in the litter beside Mistress Armstrong; the sooner we may get her to bed the better it will be. She bore the journey well, and irked us not."

"She shall have my bed upstairs; I will put on fresh linen."

The madwoman's curtains were drawn despite the heat and behind them she slept, as always, with only a slight whiffling of

179

exhaled breaths. Larkin and Penellyn carried her in, bearing her upstairs with her weight between them. Soon she was on her pillows, and Clemency fed her with broth. "She is twice the weight she might be, knowing it not," said Penellyn. His eyes were on Clemency as she brought comfort to the poor woman. "I have missed your kind ways," he said softly.

"Oh, and I yours! If you knew how the time hath seemed long . . . did you ride to the Border?"

"I did so, or I would have been with you the sooner. The Armstrongs were willing for her to come south."

"Were they strange folk?" She remembered the long-ago tale of Master John's wherein the Armstrongs were descended from a fairy and a bear. "They have a wild history," said Penellyn. "They do not regard themselves as either English or Scots, but on whichever side suits them. Their women are loaded with gold chains and jewels, for they dare not lose all to raiders."

"So the women were fair? I am jealous of them."

"You need fear no woman on this earth."

She felt his dark eyes on her, and blushed like a girl. For them to love still, as they had always loved; such magic, stronger than a fairy's! They embraced, and she rubbed her cheek against his and longed for the night. But now she must go down and greet Emma, who however had hoisted herself up behind a servant in the saddle and announced that she was going to Theale. She was smiling.

"Now David needs me no more I can be a wife to my own man again. I will be back and forth, never fear."

Emma had altered little over the years; the terse speech became her. Clemency wondered how Theale would accustom himself to having a wife again, and hoped that he would be glad.

So now they were all three beneath one roof, Penellyn, herself and Margery. Margery at first was inclined to keep herself out of the way, partly from shyness and, of course, not to intrude on their loving; but Clemency and Penellyn soon made her at ease. They would play at cards now of a night, with Larkin or one of the other servants to make a fourth at the table; but it was a merry game, not for high stakes. The trees changed colour as Clemency had known they would, and the woods from the window were for a while glorious, then sad.

Poor Margery began to thicken. She still came to church, wrapped in a warm cloak because of the season: as far as anyone knew, neighbours had not yet begun to talk. Few came to visit at Clevelys, and when they did Margery would stay upstairs and allow Clemency and Penellyn to play host. His position was less that of a steward than a member of the family, and old Larkin knew him well, liked him and was glad of his aid. Clemency would go up afterwards to relate such gossip as had been exchanged, and would find Margery seated idly before the fire, not sewing for her child as she might have done. She seldom now came down to meals; Clemency would have a manchet of bread and a platter of meats sent up to her, while she herself ate at table with Penellyn. They ate in silence, saying little to one another; their love allowed of quietness. By night they slept in each other's arms; Clemency never ceased to wonder at the delight of it, and when she awoke in the mornings, generally to find Penellyn already gone about his tasks, she would live in the warm, intimate memory of the night. By day there was Margery; and Clemency paid so much more heed to her than to herself that it was not for many weeks, when the snows came, that she wondered if her mornings were more than usually drowsy; then another wonder came. Could she, at her age, be again with child? Her courses had always continued, but she could not recall when the last had been; her mind was growing like her body, lazy and warm . . .

Penellyn came in that evening to find her bright-eyed as a girl. There was a triumphant flush in her cheeks; but for the silver hair, she looked almost like the young bride who had come long ago to Ravensyard. He said "You look well, Clemency," and stood back staring at her, as if he had never seen her before. She laughed.

"It is the candlelight," she said, "and . . . another reason, which I will tell of when you've dined."

"I cannot eat my dinner for wondering; tell me now."

So she told him; by now she was sure. He said nothing, but presently took her hands and kissed the palms, then her wrists; then his mouth was on hers, and they were happy together and full of joy. This time, she told him, he would see his child and watch it grow. "Margery is to call her boy Stephen; she asked it of me, so if ours is a boy you will have to think of a name, unless it is to be David, like yourself."

"Two Davids would make confusion. What if it is a girl? I had a soon it were, and looked as you do."

"If it is a girl I should like to call her Emma, after her aunt."

"That will please her well," he said.

She told Margery, who seemed to stir out of her lethargy long enough to say that she was pleased. Clemency kissed her. "Now your child and mine may grow together, and play and learn," she said. "There will be small difference in their ages."

"I cannot tell the future," said Margery. "It doth not seem to me that my child can be real, yet—" she laid a hand on her abdomen—"he kicks. Carrying is not so bad now as it was in the first weeks. They are the worst with sickness, until—until the labour pains, and I am afraid."

"Wait till you hold your child; it will have been worth the pain."

Margery lifted one shoulder. "It is different for you; you have known it all before."

"Not as an old woman."

"But you are not afraid, because you have Penellyn. Yet I would not that the child's father came to me now. How are they ar Ravensyard?" She did not often mention Ralph, or his house.

Clemency sat down on the settle. "Emma says there is no sign of madam's quickening, and Master Ralph is not best pleased. They do not like his wife in the kitchen; she interferes, and gives herself airs. I think he will regret you."

She spoke cheerfully, to comfort Margery; but it was like talking to a figure of wood, and her words fell empty into the air.

Lady Hawkyard died at the beginning of February, when the old often go; the roads were so slippery with rutted frozen snow that few came to the burial. Penellyn permitted Clemency to go only on his arm; he treated her now as if she were made of glass, saw that she wrapped up warmly, and would not allow her to undertake any kind of task, even about Mistress Armstrong. She laughed and protested that she did not like to be idle; but secretly she enjoyed his cherishing. They went to church, but Margery did not accompany them; she was very heavy now.

A sprinkling were there, among them Ralph and his wife, chatting in the pews nearby the coffin. Clemency did not think Ralph looked well; he was yellow and had lost weight. She had made up her mind that he should know of Margery's state other than by the sight of her, pregnant, in church; but it was difficult to speak to him alone. By good fortune, after the coffin had been borne out, he came to her, doffed his hat and bowed, and said cheerfully "How fares Mistress Margery? I had thought to see her here today; the old lady knew her well."

Clemency raised her eyes and looked levelly at him. "She cannot come in this dangerous weather; she is near her time, as you should know well enough."

He had paled. "I . . . why, I did not know."

For an instant she saw lines show in his face as though it were an old man's; she had always formerly noted him as being free of them. Then he recovered composure, turned away in silence, and rejoined his wife. May it speed ill for them, thought Clemency with malice; but at least he knows the truth, and his part in it.

Any hope, if she had nourished it, that he might show some concern for Margery's welfare, though what form it might take she did not know, was fruitless. The weather thawed at last, and in the grounds of Clevelys the snowdrops Margery's mother had long ago planted thrust tiny green spears up through the hard earth; but Margery did not walk on it. She kept to her chamber, heavy and despondent in a way that frightened Clemency; it was as though she had no will to live. She no longer attended church. Ralph must have said nothing of the matter, because there was

183

no embarrassment among neighbours and friends as to Margery's absence; they enquired for her in the usual way, not averting their eyes.

It was spring when Margery's labour pains began; the trees were bursting into tender bud. She lay on the great bed where she herself had been conceived so late, and held hard to the sheet's edge as Clemency bade her. Clemency did not leave her, though the weight of her own child was by now making her steps drag; Penellyn hovered in anxiety outside the room, less concerned for Margery, who was young and strong, than for his wife. That that young woman had known well enough what she was doing with Ralph Talmadge was his fixed opinion about Margery; but he had never said it aloud, knowing the love Clemency had for the girl who was the daughter of her oldest friends and had been married to her son. How long ago that seemed! It might have been in another age, another life, that Stephen had been born and had lived and died. His sweetheart Clare had called once, without her husband who would be busied in his office by day. She was no longer beautiful, but puffed and pale with child-birth. Gossip said Lancefolly would not leave her alone. How differently all had fallen out than the way they had foreseen it in that time past! Clemency wiped the sweat from Margery's brow with a cool rag soaked in vinegar; here am I, she was thinking, the steward's wife at Clevelys, no longer mistress of Ravensyard and hardly regretting it; yet she still grudged Ralph the house.

She came round the door to Penellyn. "Go downstairs and pour yourself wine, and some for us too," she whispered. "No, the child is not born, nor will be yet. She is in hard labour, poor soul."

"Have a care to yourself," he said, "and sit if you may." He went off and poured the wine, returning with the cups; the draught heartened Clemency, but she could not persuade Margery to sip it. The girl began to groan at last, as if the sound were forced from her against her will; up till now she had been silent. "Cry out, my dear, it will ease you," whispered Clemency, but the other might not have heard; her underlip bled from biting, and at the last she strained utterly.

The child was born and was a boy. Clemency knelt and kissed Margery's cheek. "Here is your Stephen, and he will have fair hair," she heard herself saying; the child's curls were heavy with wet, darkened to brown meantime; he would be a Talmadge.

Margery opened her pale green eyes suddenly; her gaze seemed very far away. "I am glad of you," came the breath of a whisper; it was the last time she spoke. When the women began to rub down the afterbirth she made no breaths; shortly afterwards they found that she was dead.

Clemency went to Penellyn and wept more tears than she had thought were in her. Presently he carried her up to her chamber and laid her on the bed. He unlaced her. "You are not to stir from here; I will see to everything in the house," he said. "Would you that I send for Emma now?"

Clemency nodded wearily. Now, at the lowest depth of the mind's suffering, she would be glad of Emma. Emma would lay out the body, and ensure that the wet-nurse they had already found suited the child.

That evening Ralph Talmadge came to Clevelys, face haggard beneath his hat. "I would see my son."

Clemency was not there to receive him; she slept. It was left to Penellyn to bring the baby from his nurse's arms down to the hall. Ralph gazed at the tiny features and the drying fair hair.

"He will do well with you," he said. "Had I known in time of his coming, his mother had been my wife."

Penellyn was silent. He turned away and did not wait for Ralph to leave, but heard the clatter of his horse's hooves fade into the distance, on the way back to Ravensyard.

PART THREE

ONE

If there had been no gossip during Margery's pregnancy there was plenty after her death, for it could not be concealed that she had died in childbirth; the baby Stephen thrived. However, the matter might not have been discussed openly so soon as it was had it not been for the forward manners of Ralph Talmadge's wife, Jess. She was a coarse woman, who presumed on acquaintance and interfered when she could; indeed her own life left her little else to think about, for it was known by now that her husband avoided her.

The talk came about in this way. One Sunday after service at the lych-gate, when Clemency was near her time, Jess Talmadge came up and nudged her, admiring her stomach, and saying in a loud voice "A fine man, your husband, to have sired two children at Clevelys in the space of a twelvemonth! I wish you well."

Clemency's face was scarlet; Penellyn was at some distance talking with the tenant farmers, and had not heard, but others had. She became aware that she was listened to by many pairs of ears as she replied, in a voice whose coolness did not betray her anger, "Never blame my husband, but your own, madam, for

Stephen. It is time that was known; we have kept silence on it, but I will do so no longer if it means harm to Penellyn." She looked the other in the eye. "He was in the north, madam, when Stephen was conceived; it was before your marriage; not so long before."

The other's face was the colour of a plum. "Out upon you for a lying slut! I will not have you miscall my husband."

"I am no slut, nor will I have you slander mine."

Others had drawn close to see this parley between the present lady of Ravensyard, whom no one liked, and the wife of its former steward. "Never think that I do not know of your doings," rejoined Dame Jess loudly, and she made a mocking curtsy and would have turned away. But Clemency called after her, with intent that everyone should hear, "Ask Ralph to his face if he be not the father of Margery Clevelys' son. He will scarce deny it if he values his soul."

Penellyn joined her then and she took hold of his arm, and said in a low voice "Come away quickly. There hath been that said which makes me angry, indeed." They moved away from the gate, when he said in some amusement "What, my quiet dove? Did I hear you railing like a fishwife? Methought mine ears deceived me."

"They would not have deceived you had you been nearer. The men are worse gossips than the women in this place, though there is little to choose between them."

He looked grave and said "Be sure we had great matters to occupy us. It bodes ill for England as things are. You will remember John Hampden, who was cast into prison for refusing to pay his ship-money."

"I remember it now."

"That trouble was only beginning; a war of words hath broken out between the King and commons, for he will not recall the Parliament; and who is to say whether he be right or wrong? Only he cannot govern without money, and lacking Parliament he lacks that also."

"Then why doth not he summon it?"

"Because there are many outspoken fellows in it, who would

go against the King."

The burning in her cheeks that Jess Talmadge had roused grew less, hearing of the grave matter. She looked up at Penellyn as they walked and thought again how handsome he was, far more so than any man they had left behind at the gate. He had lately grown a beard and wore it, as many did, trimmed to a narrow point; his hair was longer than it had been, and the white locks mingled together with the dark. A comely man, and gentle; would trouble come in the country to take him from her? She shivered a little, and drew close to him. "Why," he said, "you are cold."

"Only from fear of what may be. It is strange not to obey one's king."

"It hath happened earlier, and always led to war. God grant it may not be so now; they say there is a fellow named Cromwell of Huntingdon who leads the opposition and hath a great tongue in his head."

"Then they should lop it off."

"That would cause a mighty uprising. I do not envy those in places of high state. It is like walking on egg-shells."

He fell silent, and she did not even trouble him with Jess' spiteful gossip, knowing it was the kind of matter he would scorn. And at the least, she thought, the very look of little Stephen gave proof of his Talmadge parentage; he reminded her already of young Joscelyn; God had punished Ralph Talmadge in that his son so resembled his murdered nephew. God would punish the King's enemies likewise.

When her time came upon her, Clemency gave birth to a baby girl with a fuzz of fine dark hair. Her labour was easy and short, more so than when she had borne the first Stephen. She lay content, savouring Penellyn's delight in his tiny daughter when at last he was permitted to enter the room. She was able to look over at him and say "What think you of your Emma?"

"Emma," he said, savouring the name. He was touched by her question, knelt by the bed and kissed her. Clemency raised a hand to his cheek. "I love her well," he said, "and her mother also."

They were happy that year. At all seasons, through summer green and winter snow, the nursery at Clevelys was occupied greatly with babies. Clemency had found a good nurse, a kinswoman by marriage of Larkin the old steward whose husband had lately died, and she had no children of her own. From the first sight of Hannah Larkin's apple-cheeked, homely face it was evident that one might trust her with children or any other matter. The two babies were so near of an age that they were playmates as soon as they might crawl.

Happiness there was; yet some matter troubled Penellyn. At last he spoke to her of it.

"There is an ugly time coming, I fear. The King recalled Parliament, but he had better not have done so. They think to be masters of the country. If such rebels gain the upper hand there will be civil war; I cannot see any other outcome."

"Such matters are fought out only in London," said Clemency, looking out at the smooth green lawns and quiet woods. How distant trouble seemed! Already she thought of the capital as a far-off place which she had once known, where decisions on great matters were taken; they did not come to trouble country folk. "'Tis not only in London now," said Penellyn. "Sir Harry tells me that there is unrest in Scotland, where they will not observe the liturgy of Archbishop Laud. They say an old woman threw a stool at the clergyman who tried to read it in church there. That such news travels far showeth, I believe, that discontent is general. It will come to us in the end, I doubt not."

"And you?" She knew what his answer would be.

"Believe me, I do not say this to frighten you; but I shall join the King."

She had clasped her hands tightly together; below, on the grass, Hannah Larkin sat with the children, getting the sun. The scene was so peaceful, even the trees not stirring, that it was hard to believe in coming strife throughout the land. Such a thing had never happened since . . . when? Since the time they said God and His saints slept?

She shivered a little, but seeing him still watching her said quickly "Whatever you decide to do I will aid you in it. If I must, I'll steward this house myself, to leave you free to ride off as a soldier if that must be."

"You are the best wife a man ever had," he told her. "It will not be easy to leave you for any cause." But his words stayed in her mind, and she knew that their peace at Clevelys would end soon, if it had not ended already.

Ralph was dying. She had grown convinced of it by watching him week after week at church, which he would enter with Jess on his arm in her rich, vulgar clothes. He himself seemed no longer to care what he wore; he was yellow and haggard and grew increasingly more so, till he seemed like a skeleton covered with loose skin. Then he stopped coming. Jess would appear by herself, eager to seize the chance of chatting to neighbours after the service; she did not seem troubled, but Clemency doubted if she had ever had a fondness for the man she had married. With such as Jess, folk were fond of themselves; it was hardly a sin against charity to say it. Clemency and Jess never met at the church door, especially since the altercation about Stephen's parentage. In any case their acquaintance was different, and a glimpse of each other amid the throng was all either woman obtained, or wanted.

The weeks passed, and as Penellyn had foretold the news continued bad. It seemed the fashion in some circles to criticise the King; but not so here. Sir Harry Bilbee one day gave one of his broadsides. "This feller Cromwell and the rest, they'd say why do we need a king at all? This Parliament that was called hath done more harm than good; the King himself went in to arrest five members and said the birds had flown. Cromwell! They say his name was Williams in the first place, but he's kin in some fashion to that monster who lost his head in the time of Henry the Eighth. Much harm he did before that."

Clemency listened miserably to such news as she heard. Whatever befell, the days of her happiness with Penellyn and the children were numbered. It was, no doubt, a woman's view

193

that home was the world; Penellyn's gaze saw beyond it. More than ever she marvelled that he had been able to endure the long years shut away with the madwoman in the north.

But she forgot all this for the time when a strange thing happened. Ralph Talmadge sent for her, in a note brought by a servant. *I pray you come alone*, it read. *The physicians tell me I have not long to live. I would speak with you. R.*

She hesitated only briefly; Penellyn was elsewhere, and she would as soon have had his advice. But it was her duty to hear whatever it was a dying man had to tell. She flung on a hooded cloak and had a horse saddled, bidding Hannah Larkin give the children their dinner. Riding slowly lest the mount's hooves slip in the mud, she approached Ravensyard. It tugged at her heart to be close to the high wall again; a houseleek she had planted between the stones still grew. Lights shone already from the windows, which were narrow and admitted little light.

Ralph lay in bed, his face shaded by the draped curtains. When he struggled up to greet her she was shocked at how greatly he had altered even from the sick man she had last seen. There was nothing of his sleek comeliness left; his hair was white, and his skin yellow as a guinea.

"It was good in you to come," he said. "I feared you might not."

"I am sorry that you are ill," she said. He smiled a little.

"It is a disease no physician may cure. They have tried all their remedies. It is perhaps a sickness of the soul as well as the body."

She said nothing, but continued to fix her eyes steadfastly on his face. There was a smell of illness in the room; she longed to open a casement.

"Will you come to my burying, as you came to Dick's?" he asked, with a ghost of his old smile. "I know, you see, the harm he did you; he boasted of it to me long since in his cups. I made him swear silence, which I think he kept."

She had coloured deeply; her ravishing seemed as if it might have befallen another woman, so much had come between. Ralph watched her intently; he did not seem to need a reply, but

194

went on talking feverishly as though to have it all said before his strength failed. Knowing this, she kept silent; in any case there was little to say, yet one thing of which he spoke drew a cry from her.

"I have always loved you, you see, Clemency; never Alice nor Margery nor Jess."

"How can you say so?" She had withdrawn, and made as if to go; a gesture of his hand restrained her.

"Do not blame me; I knew it when I first saw you as Nick's bride, with your proud little head and its bright hair. I wanted and pitied you; well I knew Nick was no man. Yet you never liked me since I told you the tale of the Tredesc ghost, and the pair who died of starvation in the old cellar."

She remembered that; but by now she was silent with amazement. He had given no sign of loving her, indeed had acted at times as though he hated her. She stammered out something of this.

"Maybe; love turns sour if it cannot have its way, and I would never have treated you as did Dick, to whom all women were sport. In the end I married Alice so that I might have some kinship with you, and it was a fool's act, for by my so doing you became my deceased wife's sister, whom I could never have wed in the sight of the Church. And as for Penellyn—ah, well I knew who had fathered Stephen Talmadge, and for years was bitter because it was not I."

She sat very still. "Is that why you killed Stephen; from jealousy?"

"No, I killed him because I craved Ravensyard. It was my second love, and only for yourself would I have abandoned it. To steward it for many years was something; but I wanted it for mine. Over many years I planned what was to happen, especially as I watched his love grow for Clare Talmadge. There were many kinds of despair could have killed Stephen; I gambled on them all, and I bribed Burbage to help me."

She fought down revulsion: Burbage was dead. "And you killed Joscelyn . . . and seduced Margery and then left her to bear your child alone." She was still trying to fan the flames of

195

her hate; oddly, the fire had died.

"The child we will speak of later," said Ralph. "I have made provision for him. Had I known of his conception I would have married Margery. As it was, I had to do as best I might to secure myself an heir. I have fared badly, as you know."

"Because you did ill, you reaped an ill harvest." Her voice was thin and high. "I found Joscelyn's little body in the yard, despite the mist thick about it. I knew well enough then who had killed him, and by what means."

"You are my mother-confessor. All that you say is true, and yet—so heedful was I—you could never call the sheriff because you had no proof. Who could tell what had happened on a day of mist? I awaited it carefully. He and I stole out to look for the raven's nest when none could see, and the roof was slippery with wet; I despatched him easily."

"Why, why?"

"Ravensyard was not for him."

"Ravensyard . . . what harm it hath done." She moved a little. "Your son by Margery groweth more like Joscelyn each day. Had you him in the house with you—which will never be—I swear his looks would have troubled your conscience, drowsy though it seemeth. He—"

He raised a hand again. "Do not talk, my dear; I grow weaker, and I would say all to you that is to be said. We shall not meet again. Alice I poisoned, and John Talmadge too, with the foxgloves you grew in your little garden. The one was barren, and an encumbrance to me; the second only an encumbrance, to himself more than anyone."

Tears stood in her eyes; she would never be able to think of the herb-garden again without horror. "And Nick, who never harmed any? With what did you poison Nick?"

"He did harm by owning Ravensyard. I helped him on his way with, I remember, monkshood. He died quickly and almost without pain; so did the rest. Such things are commonly done for less matter than a great house. Had I my life to live again, only as a younger son, I could act no other part."

"I believe that you could not," she said slowly, then "You

wished to speak to me about the boy, your son."

"Yes. I have set matters on foot with the lawyer, Sarasin, that Stephen may be legitimised and inherit Ravensyard. As for Jess, I have left her certain liferents; she will prefer to return to town. I have named you and Penellyn as young Stephen's guardians, with an allowance for looking to him."

"We will not take it. We look to him for Margery's sake, and his home is Clevelys."

He smiled amidst his pain. "Do you tell me that you would not relish being the mistress of Ravensyard again? Fie, Clemency! It is the one thing we have both loved. You love and desire it still. I know much of you."

"And I, perhaps, of you."

"Do you hate me still?"

"The killings I cannot forgive; Joscelyn, Stephen, Alice, Nick and John, harmless souls all."

"Say then only that you will pray for my soul, as the Papists do. I have need of your prayers."

She closed her eyes for instants, remembering all her dead. Then she nodded briefly. Ralph held out his hand, wasted and showing its bones.

"I thank you for that. Will you clasp hands with me?"

Shivering, she put out her own hand and felt the dry bones grip it. Then she pulled forward her hood.

"You are going away now," he said, like a child. "It is raining; do not catch cold, Clemency."

She stood for moments looking down on him, knowing that, as he had said, they would never meet again. Suddenly his eyes opened wide and met hers. Their whites were yellowed, and the expression in them brought her near to tears. This man had loved her for years, scarcely knowing what love was; and in all her time here she had been unaware of it. Suddenly, on an impulse, she bent over and kissed his cheek. The opened eyes shone. She went quickly out.

TWO

Ralph died. After his death time seemed to swirl about Clemency and settle into a pattern, as though events were seen at the further end of a tunnel. There, in bright sunshine, she saw the children growing, Stephen's fair head close to Emma's dark one, naming the wild flowers the little girl held in her fist; then further back was darkness, and the conviction that Penellyn would not be with them for long at Ravensyard. For they were at Ravensyard again; on Ralph's death and after his widow had gone back to London, Clemency had regained possession of the heavy, ancient keys. It was not as comfortable a house as Clevelys, and folk wondered why she had returned there. She visited Clevelys sometimes, and the children rode down there on their ponies. But now they were again behind the high wall, closed off from the world; yet rumour crept in.

Rumour, and whispering; nothing yet was spoken of openly. Then one day certain news came; the King had given up the attempt to come to terms with the Parliament, other terms with the Scots; he had raised his standard at Nottingham; Oxford and not London was the centre of loyal hopes. It was civil war. Clemency knew, and dreaded, what Penellyn would do; but when the time came she was ready. She would not hinder him with tears.

"I must go, and leave you." She looked at the great height of him, the hair and beard which now were heavy with white; he was of an age when it would be no disgrace to let others fight, and stay at home. But "The King is stubborn, devious even; we all know that; but he is the King. My ancestors fought for the princes of their blood; I would be as loyal as they." And he would confer with Theale, who came up often from his ovens, and was less of a baker now than a squire to his knight; he would polish Penellyn's body-armour, fit his casque to his head, see that he had all things to hand that he needed in war. They would ride off together. Emma would do the baking afterwards. When they went, she and Clemency stood by the outer postern and waved them goodbye until there was nothing to be seen of them but dust.

She turned back to the house, her tears thick. "You will make the finest soldier of them all," she had said to him. He had come to her then and held her against him; she was reminded of their love, the happy years together, all of it; nothing could alter what they had known. She had raised her mouth to his for a last kiss, keeping her tears for when he had gone. And now the tears flowed. Afterwards she dried her eyes and went to the children. Their lives must be sheltered from this thing that had come to them all, as far it could be done.

She had letters from Penellyn from time to time. All went well at first, with a gathering of squires and gentry beneath the standard of the King. His two German nephews, Princess Elizabeth's sons, had joined their uncle, and that boded well for the war; Prince Rupert was a famous soldier already, and had ridden at breakneck speed to join the fight. There was silence after that; then news from other mouths of a great battle at Edgehill, and she was taut with fear, picturing Penellyn killed in the charge; but scrawled word came from him soon to say that it had been a victory, and that he had taken no hurt. Later he wrote proudly, to say he was become one of Prince Rupert's horsemen chosen and trained, a Cavalier. That brought her pride; he was no longer a servant, but of the blood and company of princes. She had known, since loving him, that he was no ordinary man.

For a long time after that there were brief notes only, saying he had been in a skirmish in the lanes, that Prince Rupert had disguised himself as a cabbage-seller and gone among the Roundheads to find out their news, all manner of things; everyone knew the name Roundhead now because of the rebels' cropped hair, in mockery of the King with his long tresses. Whatever befell, Penellyn seemed to take no hurt; she hoped her prayers for him wove a wreath of safety about him; yet there must be many women who so prayed and whose men were killed, maimed, taken.

She was sitting at the window one day mending Stephen's shirt, which he had torn climbing a tree, when Emma Theale came to her. Emma's hair was grey now and she had no teeth; but her spirit was as tough as ever. She said "I have never in my life been given to fancies, but the things I hear make me certain we'd be as well to prepare a place for hiding anyone should the Roundheads come; I was thinking of the cellar."

"That damp place! None could stay there and live, for long." Yet she remembered how long ago Ralph had told her of the unhappy Tredesc couple and how they had been left down there to starve. The cellar was certainly difficult to find if one did not know the house; the trap-door hid it completely. "As you say," she said, "but I pray God we need not hide our men in such a place. The war wages itself, and there are battlefields; but what danger are we in at Ravensyard? I am told the young Princes have given orders that there shall be no looting of houses or towns, and the other side must needs do likewise."

"The other side are rabble, who will loot and burn where they can, and not a country-house will be spared," replied Emma grimly. "As well make a hiding-place ready for the master and for Theale, if they should come; I can think of no better than the cellar." She walked about the room in the restless way she had and burst out "Lord! they are out for blood, and for all the Bible

201

cant they preach there will be not a one spared who hath been loyal to the King. Worcester Cathedral they left as rubble, and it will be so with many a fine house. There was much violence in the Bible; remember the woman they raped and then cut in pieces to send to all the tribes of Israel. There will be plenty of such tales of our own, mark me."

"It is our men I fear for," said Clemency. She had never grown used to the fact that London now was an enemy city; the spire of Paul's, the street-cries and the shops, were all for Cromwell's men and such as obeyed them. But that mattered nothing if only Penellyn and the children were safe . . .

Her hand crept to her throat, and fear stole upon her a little. If it came to a siege, Ravensyard was at least better fitted to prepare for it than gentle Clevelys had been. Here there was a high wall and narrow windows. She would hold out as long as might be.

Alone, she climbed the short winding stairways to tower rooms and hidden closets and passages. In the upper floor cobwebs hung like veils at corners, for it was seldom used; she could hear the shouts of the children in the garden below. Emma was growing up into a little hoyden, without her father to hinder her; how would she ever become a young lady? But meantime, there was no better place than the cellar to make ready . . . and she would board up the entrance to the roof where the ravens' nests had once been. There would be no more searching and danger there. But danger itself was all about her, at the end of the tunnel . . . If only the war were over, and Penellyn could come home!

THREE

She saw him twice, when he rode home too weary to do more
than eat and sleep and be off again; she had made the house
welcoming for him, cleaning and brushing its hangings,
washing and polishing its wood with wax from the newly tended
hives. Jess Talmadge had not cared for Ravensyard and even the
linen had all to be washed again, aired on bushes, and put away
in its chests with dried lavender from the garden as she had
always used to do. She held to her belief that one day Penellyn
would be free to savour his home again. Sometimes, when she
gave herself pause, she would lean against the wall by the newly
sparkling windows and imagine his riding to her down the road,
not tired this time but victorious; there must soon be a great
victory for the King: surely the rebels would be beaten in the
end. It could never be God's will that they should conquer.

Yet there was no great victory. Edgehill had been a hit-or-
miss affair, won by the dash and style of Rupert of the Rhine,
with his wheeling horsemen cutting a swathe through the
enemy ranks. Now, it only needed a man of genius on the
Roundhead side to train similar troops to like action: and one
had been found. His name had already been spoken of; she

recalled Sir Harry's gibe about the man's ancestor Thomas Cromwell who had lived in King Harry's time. That had been a man who had done great evil for the King, and in the end suffered. Now, this Oliver, an ugly fellow with spots and pimples, who seldom wore clean linen or a band on his hat, was heard of everywhere; not in derision, but as a greater commander of troops, if that were possible, than Rupert himself. Cromwell trained his men soberly, appealing to the innate piety of all Englishmen; where Rupert's men cursed roundly, the Model Army mouthed texts from Holy Writ, and did not disperse to plunder before a battle was won. If Oliver Cromwell were a wizard, as some had said Rupert must be, then his magic was potent. Gradually all known things changed. Little knots of people after church or outside shops in towns, or chatting to pedlars at the door, heard of such news as might have come. But there was no victory for the King, only a defeat at a place with a bleak name; Marston Moor.

Clemency could not eat or sleep till she had word from Penellyn that he was safe. He said little of himself, however, and seemed more concerned with his master. *The Prince's white dogg Boye, which followed him always, was killed by Gunshot in the battle. It will hearten the Rebels, who said it was a Familiar who gained us Victory. The Prince is much cast down. I am safe, thank God, except for a little Scratche, and Theale also. My love and Harte to you.* She worried about the little scratch; no doubt it was more serious than he said, but at least he was able to write and, no doubt, to mount his horse again. She lived from day to day; there were Roundhead victories at Newbury and in the north, and later Oxford was besieged because it was the King's headquarters and had always been a loyal city. Several wives were with their husbands there and Clemency longed to be near Penellyn; but there were the children, and whatever other women did she would not leave Stephen and Emma in the care of servants.

For a long time there was a complete lack of news; she had no idea where Penellyn might be. Then, like an ill wind, there came filtering down from the north news of a great Roundhead victory. Again a scrawled note came from Penellyn, written beforehand. *They say there is to be a great Bataille in this place, and God knoweth how the Day will fare. I am glad you are not with the Wives and Camp Followers that are behind us; keep safe at Ravensyard. My Love and Harte.*

The place was called Naseby. There were to be other battles, other forays and attempts to make peace; but there the King's cause had met its death-blow.

That had been in summer. No news came, and Clemency made herself accept the fact that Penellyn must be dead, lying with so many others on that fatal field of humps and spinneys, awaiting burial. Yes, others had lost husbands and lovers besides herself; she must think of them, and of the children. She was not the only woman in England to mourn. But what now was to become of England, and of all those who were left?

Two children on ponies, a fair boy and a girl with elf-locks of dark hair escaping beneath her hat, galloped about the deserted bridle-paths of Clevelys among the turning leaves of bronze and flame and gold. They were still in sight of the gate with its massy pillars of sun-soaked brick and the white stone griffins that guarded either side; their laughter could be heard on the wind. The girl was teasing the boy, who flushed easily under his delicate skin.

"My pony is smaller than yours, and I myself am smaller than you. Yet I can easily beat you, Stephen. Are you not shamed that such a thing should be?"

She wheeled away, setting her mount at a low hedge; and Stephen thought it his duty to follow, for Aunt Clemency had bidden him strictly to have charge of Emma, who was wild in her ways. This was so much so that even their new tutor, whom no one liked and who whipped them too often, could not tame her. He set his mount at the same hedge. The beast jibbed, and Emma broke into mocking laughter which was borne backwards on the wind. How often in his life Stephen would have to endure that laughter! In due time, and long after marriage,

Emma's wild-rose beauty was to catch the eye of that experienced monarch and squire of dames, King Charles the Second; and perhaps there was a premonition in this day when she teased and chased and eluded Stephen all over the green grass and between the bright sad trees that lined the paths they rode.

Stephen, who liked to ponder, took time to think of Master Lanson, their tutor, from whom they had escaped this day with Aunt Clemency's blessing. He knew that she did not like the tutor, who had been sent to replace Master Gunning, whom they had liked and with whom they learned well. It had something to do with Master Lancefolly, who had reported in high places that Master Penellyn, Emma's father, had gone to fight for the King. One day the new tutor had appeared with a letter, keeping his eyelids down above his sour-milk face. Gunning had gone from Ravensyard, and Lanson was left in his stead. It was a pity.

He called aloud to Emma. "Lanson will fume at us when we return. Had we not better go home now?" He always deferred to her, and cursed himself for doing so; she was a girl, after all; but already she had enchanted him and she was the master, not he.

"Lanson may fume all he likes. You know who sent him: Lancefolly, who gives his wife a baby a year, and all of them mim as milk. I know how babies come. So do not you, Master Stephen Prettyface. You should have been a girl and I a man. It is strange how the Lord disposeth of us." She had learned, he knew, to speak of the Lord from Lanson, who seldom had the word out of his mouth. But it was time they were home; Aunt Clemency would be anxious. As for babies, the thought filled him with confusion. There were many things Emma knew more of than he. Who had told her about babies? Perhaps it was Aunt Emma Theale, who never minced her words. At any rate, it was time they were going.

"Look there," said Emma.

A great cart had come up, laden with autumn turnips. A poor woman drove the broken-down horse, her hat of soiled felt tied on with an old dirty kerchief. She brandished a whip at the gateway, and called to the children to ask if any were at home.

"My mother is at Ravensyard, but she doth want no turnips,"
Emma called impudently. The woman however turned her cart
and plodded on up the hill. "Why doth she trouble to go when
we have enough of our own, and I told her so?" asked Emma.
She was a knowing little baggage, and could tell anyone anything about the estate and farms. Stephen stared after the
departing cart, and said nothing. He pulled at his beast's rein
and returned to the bridle-paths, late as it was. "I will race you
to the pond," he said.

"I can beat you to the pond and back. You are a slow rider,
Stephen; you think too much."

"And you think too little." But they raced one another down
the paths, and drew dead level while the turnip-cart trundled on
towards Ravensyard.

The cart drew up outside the wall. A groom saw it, and called
across that they did not need fodder. "I would have a word with
the lady of the house," replied the driver, head bent.

"Madam is occupied."

"Then send Emma Theale."

The groom went off in surprise. Presently Emma came out
and received a wink from the driver. "Say naught," he whispered. "There is a great load under these turnips."

Emma was quick. "Where can we hide him? God knows,
there's eyes everywhere since that tutor came." She put her
hand to her bosom and recalled the cellar.

"Dame Clemency will know of a place," said Theale meantime. "Tell her, and get me leave to drive round to the back of
the yard. I can leave the cart there and unload when 'tis dark."

"How will he fare? Is he wounded?"

"Ay."

She hurried off, and presently Clemency, very pale, came
down in her cloak and hood. She had just been about to ride off
to Bilbee to ask for Sir Harry, who these days was queasy and ill.
She was fearful lest the tutor follow. That he had orders to spy
on them she knew; if it must be, she would capture him with
talk while Emma and Theale hid Penellyn. But, oh, to see

Penellyn again!

She came to where Theale sat in his woman's clothes and said loudly "Yes, I will take the turnips. Emma, you and this woman unload them; the men have their duties." So the cart was taken round to the back, where few went. She closed her eyes; the anguish of living with the near certainty that Penellyn was dead had drained all hope from her; now, it was like the thawing of a numbed limb, and he was not yet out of danger. Many would have heard no more since Naseby and its littered graves. Afterwards—how long it seemed!—she was to hear how Theale had saved himself and his master.

"There was a spinney there, and a great drift o' dead leaves up against a tree bole. I clawed at 'em and later carried *him*, the Lord knows how, and bleeding he was, in there and buried him under the leaves and myself with him. Later we heard the Roundhead devils come, laughing and talking their Bible cant—they'd been to the women by then—and they thrust their pikes this way and that, and grazed me where I lay, but hurt him none; he'd been hurt enough as 'twas. He left his right arm on Naseby field, Dame Clemency; with Rupert's own band he was, and they say the Prince himself had to take horse and fly back to Market Harborough. 'Tis strange that he taketh no wound, as though magic sat upon him. But a-many of ours were wounded, and many dead."

"But that was in summer. Where have you been?" Clemency turned her head in the light of the lantern to watch Penellyn as he lay on the pallet they had made ready in the cellar; it was night, and the house was quiet. They had kept him under the piled turnips till nothing could be seen from the windows, then hurried him past the iron trap-door and down. White of face he was, appearing more dead than alive; discoloured bandages covered the place where his arm had been. Her kisses and tears had not wakened him. The turnips had served their purpose and lay now in a heap in the yard. We are so watched, she thought, that enquiry may be made even about that; I'll have the men shift them to the fields tomorrow, and the cart can go.

She went to where Penellyn lay, holding and warming him,

while Theale told her briefly about the noblewoman who had sheltered them. "Her own lord was slain, and instead of grieving she took in many of our men and many poor women, slashed in the face and bleeding as they were after the brutes' foray into the baggage train. Without her I doubt my master would not ha' lived; she dressed his wound and cared for it, and all the rest."

"What is her name? I must write to thank her greatly."

"Best not; it might bring trouble on her and on those she still shelters, who were not ready to be got away. Noll Cromwell's spies are everywhere now, and a letter not safe."

"I know that well; we have one in the house. He is occupied with the children, or he might well have followed us. He maketh reports to his masters how things go on here."

She set Penellyn back gently on his pillows. "Would he take some broth, think you? Emma, do you go and fetch it, and take care . . ."

Emma went. "He dare not lie here long, lady," said Theale. "Of a surety they will have word, and be here soon to search. There is not a great house in four counties but hath suffered as soon as they thought the master be home; much looting there hath been, and—and oft-times worse." His red face darkened in the unsteady light. "Where else may we put him?" said Clemency. "We made this ready long ago." This cellar where a man and his wife had once starved to death was damp, and mouldy; could a sick man grow well here? Theale shook his head; she noted the authority that had come upon him now his master was ill.

"He must be got overseas, mistress. England is no place for the King's men now, nor will be till with God's grace wrong be put right."

Clemency smoothed Penellyn's hair. She would bring clean linen and dress his stump when he had eaten; no one else should do that. He murmured a little against her shoulder; presently his one hand groped for hers. She took it and held it tightly, saying in a soft voice "You are home now, my dearest, home. You are at Ravensyard." But he did not reply, though he seemed to know she was with him; after he had had a few spoonfuls of the broth he seemed to fall into a natural sleep. She watched by him as long as she might; in the end she had to leave, because of the man Lanson who would join them at supper. How was she to sit at table as though nothing had occurred, and listen to his prosy talk? Yet it had to be done.

She left Penellyn with Theale and blankets, candles and food. When it was late, and the tutor slept, she and Emma would come in turn again.

She had dared send for no physician, though as the days passed Penellyn seemed to gain strength and awareness; but he was still very weak. Since the Cromwellian victory officers had begun to be installed in the towns, keeping watch on all the inhabitants. Here, their own Rector had been displaced from the church living and a canting Presbyterian put in his place. Were she to stay quiet at Ravensyard and cause no stir, might Penellyn be left in peace in his sad cellar till he was well? She could only hope for it. She turned to the Theales and smiled at them despite her tear-stained face.

"Lacking you both, what should I have done?" she said. "It is thanks to you that he lies here and not below ground."

Whenever she could she would go to Penellyn, combing his hair and bathing his face and body with warm water for his ease. Theale had shaved the beard from him lest he be recognised as a King's man, and the stubble stood out greyly. By now he certainly knew where he was, and spoke to her; but he was weary almost to death, and she gave him draughts of poppy-seed to make him sleep. With that, and the nursing and food, and her presence, he improved slowly. There had been problems otherwise; what to do with the broken down mare, which dare not be left in the stables? Best perhaps to turn her loose in the fields to graze, or would it be safer to shoot her and bury the carcass? Yet she had done good service, and someone, somewhere, might have need of her as Theale and Penellyn had done. In the end they put her in the clover-field, where she grew sleek by winter. But before then, many things had come about at Ravensyard.

Clemency had bad news soon enough. A little maidservant, weeping and dishevelled, hammered at the door; they had come, she said, a great many armed men, and had looted Clevelys, but as there was no owner present had spared the house. "They are on their way to you here, mistress, but I ran across by the field path." A sergeant, she thought he was, with papers, was among them.

Clemency gave her money and bade her hasten home to her parents. "If you are found here, child, they will blame you, and I would not have that happen."

"God in His mercy keep you, mistress!" The girl was gone, the sound of her running footsteps fading in the distance. In the quiet which fell, Clemency waited. She would hear the soldiers before she saw them; their clumping booted feet, the horses' trampling hooves, the shouting of orders.

They came. In the midst of waiting she had said to herself that there had been brave women in this war, who had held their houses at siege. Ravensyard had such a wall. They might scrabble up stones from the yard and hurl them down, perhaps holding off the helmeted men for awhile; they had food to last; but it was not wise, with the traitor Lanson in the house and the wounded men to defend. Best let them come in peace, and perhaps, with the spoiling of Clevelys, they would be glutted and take no more.

So she was waiting at the inner door for them, after they had defiled uphill and past the wall entry. The sergeant was a red-faced man, tall and with the broad vowels of the north. He shouted at her as soon as he was within distance.

"You are Clemency Penellyn?"

She nodded to the disrespectful salutation. The man looked her up and down, evidently expecting her to cringe with fear; as she did not, he regained some measure of courtesy.

"Where is your husband?"

"Fighting for his King."

The men murmured, and the officer cut in harshly. "The

traitor Charles Stuart hath suborned many, and I know your husband was among them. But the land is differently governed now, praise God. I have word that your man was brought here, this way, not long since, and may well be in your house."

"One of your own men, Lanson, is in my house; it would hardly hold him and my husband."

"So, you are stiff-necked. I believe we may show you otherwise. If you will lead me to Penellyn, I will spare your house and chattels. If you do not, I have fire and mangonels; your house shall burn, not one stone being left upon another for the abomination that you are, Jezebel."

She did not answer, and presently was shoved roughly against the wall while the men stormed into the house. Lady, little Emma's pet spaniel, was in the hall and crept forward trustfully; one of the foremost men gave her a kick in her soft belly, and she yelped with pain. Emma, who had escaped to the gallery, broke forth and stormed downstairs to save her darling. She seized the dog and, unafraid, railed at the men, who laughed aloud. "See what a vixen we have here!" called one, and spitted the dog on the point of his sword and bore it away, bleeding. Emma screamed and began to cry; the poor dog howled, and the men made an end of it, shortly cutting its throat. "Pert maids should be taught who's master," said one to the child, who was sobbing uncontrollably. Clemency fought her way to the little girl and turned the dark head into her skirts. "Hush, sweetheart, do not look," she said, and kept her arms about Penellyn's daughter.

"They have hurt Lady—it was horrid, wicked—"

"She is not in pain now, darling. Hush, do not anger them. You shall have another dog, I promise."

"I want only Lady. Another dog will not be like her."

"Enough of this," said the sergeant curtly. The men were stabbing and ripping at everything in the hall, as though they searched behind hangings and under benches for what they sought. Clemency tried to comfort Emma and at the same time keep her own thoughts clear. How well would Penellyn's concealment serve? If they set the house afire, the dungeons

212

would not burn, nor would the nearby flagged passages. Yet the smoke from such a fire might well smother him where he lay. She thanked God Theale was with him; one hale man was an asset, and Theale's wits were sharp. Otherwise she could only pray. She smoothed Emma's hair, and was thankful neither of the children knew of Penellyn's presence in the house. Perhaps in the madness of their destruction the men would not take time to look for a trap-door. It was in a dark place, and might not show to a casual searcher. These men were so inflamed one would think they were drunk if it were not for the known godliness of Oliver's followers, who could torture and kill a child's pet in her sight. They must not find Penellyn.

Later they tried to question little Emma, and Stephen also, who was brought downstairs by Master Lanson. They made close enquiry of Stephen; he was the older, and might have been expected to know more. But he told them nothing, because he could not. The tutor stood with eyes downcast, offering help to no one. He might have been removed from the events which surrounded him; at any rate it was unlikely that he knew any of the soldiers, his life having been studious.

Emma gave them short answer. "You hurt my dog, and I hate you," was all she would say. Clemency tried to hush her, fearful of their anger, but it made matters worse. "If my father were here, he would fight you and kill you," said Emma, "because of what you did to Lady. And I would laugh while you died."

"Why, Master Tutor," said the sergeant, "I would prescribe a sound whipping for a forward little wench."

"That shall not be," said Clemency quietly. The men had gone on to search the rest of the house. Her heart felt cold with fear, but there was no yell of triumph to say they had found the dungeon. If she had known, Theale hung with the whole of his weight on the ladder that led down from the door; they would not wrench it up. Presently they came back. Clemency took a moment to stare at her house; everything in it was ruined, the pewter kicked and stamped upon, the benches marked with sword-cuts, the tapestries ripped. She almost felt laughter rise; they might do what harm they would, provided Penellyn kept safe. Amazement came to her amid the sounds of looting; had not Ravensyard been her pride, her only love, for years? Now it was worth far less than one man's life, if that man were Penellyn.

Later she was to learn that they had rushed into the bedchamber where poor Kate Armstrong lay, and hearing her breathe thought there was a man hidden there. They tore open the curtains and thrust their small-words in as she lay, spitting her like a fowl; the blood began to seep into the bed-linen, and Kate died with her mouth open, as though she would scream. They passed through the room, as she was not what they sought; and went into the others, tearing, cutting, destroying; then came back empty-handed.

The officer turned an angry face on Clemency. "Now, for your stiff-necked obstinacy you shall see your goods rise in flame. Hell's heat is for godless folk; I doubt not you will have your share. The Lord is on our side, as He hath shown abundantly; and we will have Penellyn yet, wherever you have despatched him."

"You have a strange way of thanking the Lord." She thought it best to keep her temper up; they must not guess at the gladness in her heart. At the least, there was hope still.

"Hold your tongue," said the sergeant. "A scold merits a ducking, and a harlot slashed ears." She fell silent; that was what had happened to the women after Naseby.

The soldiers had found bales of dry hay in the stables, and on to this they ladled dripping and butter from broken store-crocks. Clemency found her cloak and put it on, wrapping the children round on each side; soon they would be out in the night, with nowhere to go till these devils had gone. After that they might shelter at Clevelys; it still had a roof. She saw Master Lanson the tutor standing about and called to him, in a tone she might have used to a scullion, "Go from here; I would not have your company any more than the devil's." He took himself out of the way, but she doubted if she was rid of him for good.

The grease-laden hay began to crackle and smoke spread

through the hall. From somewhere, she heard the maidservants screaming; presently Emma Theale came out—without panic, good Emma—and told her that the kitchens had been cleared of folk. "Say naught," Clemency told her in a low voice. "They will be watching us, even afterwards."

Afterwards. It would be a life without Ravensyard. She felt curiously aloof as the timbers began to smoulder, not quickly by reason of their age. Much of the first flame had been dissipated, but if she had hoped to evade destruction she had deceived herself. Some of the men left, and presently there was a heavy thudding as the mangonels took aim from below the hill. "Let us go," said Clemency. As they went, they saw the outer wall start to crumble with the repeated slingsful of great stones shot at it. It had begun to grow dark, and soon the brightness of flame and patched shadow mingled to weave a tapestry of madness among them; even the men's faces seemed inhuman in the orange half-light. The smell of burning wood, cloth and feathers came; then there was a stench of singeing flesh. Clemency felt her heart leap with terror. Emma Theale drew close to her in the darkness, and told her what had happened to Kate. Clemency began to sob. "Poor soul, I had forgot her," she said. "Nick's mother, and I gave her no more heed than a beast. We should have brought her down by some means, and saved her." Tears ran down her face mingled with the soot of the fire; she looked like a distraught woman. Emma soothed her.

"Why, her life was a burden to her, or rather no life; better that she should go, and they thinking they had found others, which they had not."

"Say naught. They may still be listening. I shall blame myself to my life's end that I did not take thought to her."

"They will not hear," said Emma. The roaring of the fire in the nearer part of the house was loud, and every now and again would come a further load of shot, sending a shower of worked stones falling down the hillside. They stood at a safe distance in a field; Clemency was praying. It might be that the fire would not touch him where he was and to this hope she clung. The soldiers would not leave till, as they had said, not one stone stood upon another; but they had spared the stone floors because they must. There might be red-hot rubble to dig through on the morrow, but any who watched could think that they searched for crockery, jewellery, such things as might have survived the fire.

In the end the men left. All through the long night Clemency waited, with Emma Theale by her side, praying for their men; the children and servants had been sent to Clevelys. Once she knew terror when the flames rose and swayed, as if they would take control after all, but they sank at last to a lurid glow which might be seen across country. Stone was no food for them. A light warm wind came, fanning the sinking fire awhile; in the east, at last, there was promise of sunrise. For the first time in her life, from here, Clemency had a clear view of the trees beyond Ravensyard now that the smoke had died. There was no house left to bar it.

FOUR

"You must not go there; you must not be seen to be near. It is better for me to go, and if any should ask I will tell them that I am searching for Theale's oven, which may have survived."

Dully, she heard Emma Theale, who seemed to have taken upon herself the authority which should have been Penellyn's or Clemency's own. She was grateful to Emma and to Theale, everlastingly so. The forlorn, chilled group of women and children had gathered at Clevelys, which although robbed still stood. It was Emma who had collected enough in the way of covers to enable her, Clemency, to lie down on a ripped bed with little Emma by her, passing the dawn hours too exhausted to sleep.

What had become of Penellyn and Theale? Could a wounded and sick man, even with a companion to aid him, have survived beneath the holocaust at Ravensyard? She had pictured, fearfully, in her own mind everything that might have happened; suffocation in the smoke, slow despair and death at the end; torture in the heat. The iron trap-door and the ladder would have been red-hot with the flames nearby; it would have been like roasting alive. If only there had been clear air through the tiny grid which acted as window! If only Penellyn might have life still she would pay the penalty, that they might never meet again; and she knew that had she the chance, once more, of the life of the house and that other precious life, her reply would be the same.

The soldiers had gone off again on their plundering forays; she knew well enough that Lanson the tutor would return. He was no less than an official spy, of a kind imposed now on every Royalist household. It was mostly women and children who were left, but they must be watched constantly and reported on, lest they send money or help to their lords in hiding or abroad. "Many have fled to Holland and France," she heard herself saying, as if instructing her own mind in what it knew too well already. Somehow, if Penellyn lived, this country, no longer safe for him, must be abandoned; not even the mountains of Wales would hide him. He must be shipped aboard a vessel, but how? Who could aid him in reaching a port?

"If you find them alive what will you do?" she faltered to Emma Theale. "He dare not come here; they would burn Clevelys as Ravensyard, and have him as well."

Emma reached in her cloak and brought out a long thin piece of rusted metal. "It is a file," she said to Clemency's bewilderment. "If they live—and do not hope for it, Clemency—there are those who may smuggle our men out, that I know of. I will not tell you more; it is better so."

"Will I see him again?" If he were dead, her own life was at an end; she would go on as she must, caring for the children at Clevelys, by steps refurbishing and repairing the house; administering Stephen's estate which still stood firm under his father's will. But she would be a shadow of herself, a wraith who longed to be dead with Penellyn. How cruel a thing love was when it must be denied! Not to see him daily, to know that others besides herself dressed his hurts, and comforted him; that was the hard way, but Emma was right.

"I do not know. I may not come back, for if they are alive I must take them away. I will leave a sign for you, and later send word if I may. There is a great willow in the copse below

218

Ravensyard; you know the one?" She knew; it was nearby the willow that Dick had raped her. "I will strip a piece of bark," said Emma. "When you see the peeled wood, you will know he is safe on his way, and Theale also."

"God go with you, Emma. Here is money." She still carried silver in her purse which hung at her belt, for the soldiers had not laid hands on her. "Here," she said again, and thrust it into Emma's hands. "Use it as you think best, and if *he* doth not need it, then for yourself and Theale. And let me know how you fare, for you deserve well of me; there will be more money from the lawyers." What was left of her own marriage portion would, she thought, be sent overseas if they won there; but if she herself were to try to go the Cromwellians would not let it leave the country. They said that for this cause the Queen herself lived in poverty in France.

Emma left, and to occupy her mind Clemency turned to the children. Little Emma still sobbed over the loss of Lady; to a child such things meant everything; may she never, thought Clemency, know what it is to lose a man. How little the child had seen of her own father! Penellyn had had small joy of his children; now, they might never see him again.

She turned away, for her own thoughts screamed at her; she could picture Emma Theale scrabbling among ashes that were still warm, searching for a grid through which there might come no answer. She would not know till she went to the willow; and she dared not go so soon.

The day passed, and they cooked food on a fire they built out of fragments of the charred wood of Clevelys' great table, fashioned in the days of Edward the Third. Clemency could not eat; she drank a little water, for there was no wine, but during the day Sir Harry Bilbee sent over two great cheeses, and flagons, and word that they were to come to him if nowhere else sheltered them. Before going, Clemency went down to the willow; her heart was in her mouth at what she might find. If there was no mark, then all hope was gone. They might have arrested Emma Theale, with a watch set.

They had not. There, in the bark, was a neatly cut oblong. If she were to go to the Ravensyard grid it would be filed away. They had been rescued, Theale and Penellyn, but how had Emma contrived alone? Thank God for the brave woman. She would learn more in time. Had they lifted Penellyn, the pair of them, out through the filed grating without hurt? But she must not think, she must not ask, yet. Theale and his wife knew of devious ways, perhaps learned during the years when she was with her brother in the north and they exchanged word through pedlars, whom Theale never sent away without hot new bread. She had heard since then that some pedlars were priests, bringing the sacraments to those who practised the ancient Catholic Faith in secret. Perhaps some such help had been forthcoming. How little she knew!

She had been right; there were friends, though not from the quarter she had thought of. In a few days there came a gipsy woman to the door of Clevelys, propped as it was with wood till its hinge be mended. The woman was selling pegs. Clemency met her. The dark eyes looked steadily out from under a faded hood and she said "I have word for the mistress of Ravensyard."

"I am she, but there is no house there now; we live here, as you must know who found us."

"We know many things; it is faster to send word by us across the hills than by a rider on a horse." She drew a soiled piece of paper from her bodice and handed it to Clemency. Her fingers trembled as she opened it. Penellyn's handwriting was unrecognisable; he had spelt out the letter laboriously with his left hand. *I am safe, tho' somewhat the worse for the Heat*, it read. *There are Friends here who will see me safe on a ship to France, from where I dare not say lest it put them to Questioning. Ann who brings this will tell you where you may See me, if you will come.*

A cold short note, to give no hint of his identity or anyone else's. She said to the woman "You are Ann?"

"Ann Faa."

"May I go with you? Have you eaten? One of our men shot rabbits, and we are having them for dinner, and there is wine."

"Do not be seen to treat one of us so, or it will be reported. If you would come, fetch your cloak."

She had no one she dared tell but young Stephen, and she sent for him and put her hands on his shoulders. "I am going away," she told him. "It will not be for long, and if any ask you must say I have gone to Ravensyard to see if aught remains. If they ask further, say you know nothing. Guard little Emma for me. The tutor may come back; do not give him trouble, lest he bring the soldiers again."

He listened quietly, gravely; then nodded. She might have been talking to a grown man, not the son of Margery and Ralph Talmadge. She kissed him and went.

They walked together, she and the gipsy woman, for two hours, taking paths no horse had trodden. When dark began to fall Clemency found the twigs of trees brushing her face; the ground was uneven and she often stumbled. What a secret country was hidden in their own! These folk knew how to conceal themselves, and others.

She laughed a little, remembering how, long ago, Dame Joan Talmadge had made her afraid of the Egyptians at the back of the market tent, thinking they had been bribed to make off with her. Maybe they had. She said to Ann Faa "I will give you silver often, for this thing you are doing for us. I do not have it by me, but I will not forget; come to Clevelys later, and ask for me."

"Master Theale was good to us," said Ann. She raised an arm and pointed to where, between the crowding trees, a fire could be seen. Soon they came out into a clearing, where several men sat, some making brooms. There was a good smell of stew from a cauldron cooking on the fire; its steam was fragrant with herbs. Clemency found that this smell of cooking game, the smell of woodsmoke, of dogs and of tobacco, clung to everything in the gipsy camp. A thin lurcher sidled towards them and, seeing Ann, raised its head, eyes glowing in the dark. The woman went to where a bearded man sat smoking, and said a few words to him; he nodded.

"I am to take you to them," she said, returning. Clemency followed her to where the dark shapes of covered carts stood;

lights shone from them. She was led to where her husband lay, on a bed of rushes with ragged covers over him, and a lantern. Theale sat by him, but at Clemency's coming touched his hat, and went out, saying "He is better."

She had brushed past Theale, and knelt down, putting her arms about Penellyn. For some moments neither spoke; his single arm encircled her, and his mouth, in the old way, sought her hair. It was enough to kneel here by him, to know that he was mending, for a while; at last she spoke to him.

"You were burned," she said. His skin had the dull redness of recent hurt, and his hand and fingers were blistered. He smiled.

"It will mend. Ann Faa's mother knows of cures. They are ready for whatever may befall; if the camp is threatened they will say there is plague in it. But folk seldom see them."

"I bless them from my heart. How did you fare in the cellar, when . . ."

"Why, we were like St Lawrence on his gridiron, a little. Theale clung to the bars of the grid to try to force them apart, but only burnt his hands. Both of us stayed near it, to have air to breathe. Then it was over and Emma came with her file, and then told these folk whom she knows well, and they reached us and, somehow, got me through the opening we had made, and carried me here."

"And you are mending. I do not think God would have let me find you in the north only to lose you now. I will pray for your safe passage."

Penellyn smiled. "Pray for a calm sea." His eyes devoured her face. "It is hard to think that my safety means losing you, my heart."

"When you are safe overseas, I will come to you sometimes, with money." There would, she knew, be no occupation for a man with a missing limb. She remembered how long ago his deft fingers had swept the Welsh harp, and her eyes filled with tears.

"I will live for your visits, Clemency. Do not weep."

She was already planning them; she would tell her household,

222

so that Lanson the tutor heard it, that she was going to London, to Aunt Talmadge; and instead she would slip abroad a vessel with such gold as she might carry about her. And they would write to one another; and one day, when the King should enjoy his own again, they would live together at Clevelys, contentedly. They would be old then; it mattered nothing.

Soon Ann Faa came to say it was time to be going back, while the moon shone. Clemency laid her mouth against Penellyn's for a long kiss; she made herself smile through her tears.

"God go with you, my dear. Till we meet again, farewell. Let Theale look well to you, as I cannot."

"He will not fail," he said, "nor will you. The thought of you hath been my pride and stay; God bless you, Clemency."

They had not spoken of Ravensyard; it no longer mattered.

Next day, knowing he would have gone, she took an ash stick and made herself walk to where the house had stood. The ashes and ruins were spread over an acre of ground above the hill. Not even a wall had been left standing; there seemed nowhere to shelter a mouse. But as she watched, a strange thing happened. A great black raven, such as had used to come here, alighted, and cocked its head and beady eyes. She stood still, watching it, remembering Nick and his pet raven; remembering many things. She did not think that she would ever come here again, but the evil had gone; presently the raven flapped its wings and flew away. Perhaps it had been searching for a nest when spring should come. She stared after it till it was out of sight, then made her way slowly back to Clevelys.